What the critics are saying…

"…Annie Windsor captivates as never before with more danger, more excitement, more mind-blowing sex…the best of passion, danger, intrigue…HOT and a blast. It will leave you breathless!" ~ *Tracey West, Road to Romance*

"…An exciting, sexy sequel to The Sailmaster's Woman…Kudos to Ms. Windsor on another engrossing, one-sitting read!" ~ *Denise Powers, Sensual Romance*

"…Superb, topping its magnificent predecessor… "Definitely one for the keeper shelf." ~ *Sharyn McGinty, In The Library Reviews*

Arda: The Sailkeeper's Bride

Annie Windsor

ARDA: THE SAILKEEPER'S BRIDE
An Ellora's Cave Publication, April 2005

Ellora's Cave Publishing, Inc.
1337 Commerce Drive, Suite #13
Stow, Ohio 44224

ISBN #1419950517

ARDA: THE SAILKEEPER'S BRIDE
Copyright © 2003 Annie Windsor
Other available formats: ISBN MS Reader (LIT), Adobe (PDF),
Rocketbook (RB), Mobipocket (PRC) & HTML

Edited by: *Ann Richardson*
Cover art by: *Christine Clavel*

Warning:

The following material contains graphic sexual content meant for mature readers. *Arda: The Sailkeeper's Bride* has been rated *E-rotic* by a minimum of three independent reviewers.

Ellora's Cave Publishing offers three levels of Romantica™ reading entertainment: S (S-ensuous), E (E-rotic), and X (X-treme).

S-ensuous love scenes are explicit and leave nothing to the imagination.

E-rotic love scenes are explicit, leave nothing to the imagination, and are high in volume per the overall word count. In addition, some E-rated titles might contain fantasy material that some readers find objectionable, such as bondage, submission, same sex encounters, forced seductions, etc. E-rated titles are the most graphic titles we carry; it is common, for instance, for an author to use words such as "fucking", "cock", "pussy", etc., within their work of literature.

X-treme titles differ from E-rated titles only in plot premise and storyline execution. Unlike E-rated titles, stories designated with the letter X tend to contain controversial subject matter not for the faint of heart.

Also by Annie Windsor:

Arda: Sailmaster's Woman

Equinox

The Legacy of Prator: Cursed

Redevence: The Edge

The Legacy of Prator: Redemption

Cajun Nights

Arda: The Captain's Fancy

Vampire Dreams

Ellora's Cavemen: Tales from the Temple IV

Arda: The Sailkeeper's Bride

To:

My precious family, especially my Manysouls. Without your help, I'd be nothing, and nowhere.

Special thanks to my critique partner Cheyenne. You keep me in line.

Prologue

Ki Tul'Mar hadn't struggled as the *Ord'pa* forced his neck to the chopping block and chained him to the loop on its surface—but he struggled now to see the fireworks in the Eastern sky.

The battle had come planetside, and this gave even the die-hard law followers pause. Some were thinking to let the Sailmaster live a few moments longer, if only to turn back this threat.

Akad was certainly of this mind. Of course, Akad had been doing everything within his priestly powers to draw out the execution.

Ki was grateful, until the moment he could no longer sense his wife, his child, or his sister. Thinking so many of his heart's family dead, he wanted to die himself—but then the stars caught fire.

And Ki thought he caught a glimmer of Elise's life force.

Forcing his way to his feet, pulling at the chopping block's ring with his bull's neck, Ki snarled at the red-robed *Ord'pa*. The poor lesser priest stepped back, even though he was armed with a double-bladed axe and every muscle in Ki's body wore a chain.

Reaching his thoughts to all available *pa*, Ki located a crashing speeder. With lives inside. He couldn't read them well—Elise, but not Elise. Krysta, but not Krysta. And another. Primitive, yet not primitive.

Not bothering to sort it out, Ki flung almost the full force of his psi power into slowing the ship's descent. He left only enough energy to keep the Fleet sailing. The rest went to his task.

In his mind's eye, the blazing bubble of pa skimmed treetops, coming closer—and then his actual eyes could see it. A twisted, mangled piece of a speeder.

The crowd gasped and murmured.

Ki guided the flaming bubble to a halt above the Tuscan clearing, and lowered it to the ground beside the Platform.

Immediately, the priests and witnesses set about putting out the flames, using coats and psi power and what water could be had.

Akad leaped off the platform and waded into the ruined ship—but quickly ran back out again, screaming like a hog at slaughter.

This caused the *Ord'pa* to raise his horrid axe beside Ki.

At that moment, the crowd around the speeder fell away. Many yells and shouts could be heard, and then Ki saw the reason.

A woman came stalking from a rent in the dead ship's side, wielding a great emerald sword above her head.

But not just any woman.

Ki's mouth fell open in wonder.

Lorelei. By the Gods. The Lorelei have come!

Her clothes were torn and smoking, leaving her barely clothed. Great tendrils of pa marked her hands, arms, chest and face, ending in stark flame patterns about her smudged, desperate eyes.

And yet, this wild woman looked and felt familiar. The curve of her hips. The grace of her walk. The wild abandon of her moon-kissed blond tresses.

Elise. It had to be Elise.

And yet...not. She was changed. Different.

As she approached, Ki realized that somehow, Elise had merged with pa, like a true Ardani. Raw pa had touched her, and yet instead of burning her or killing her as it would most primitives—or at best touching her and fleeing when put down—the universe's life force had joined with her flesh and spirit.

How could this be?

More screaming filled the clearing, this more untamed than the bestial noises coming from Elise.

Another naked female left the smoldering wreck. This one was firehaired and pale, but also covered in magnificent *pa* designs. She held not one sword, but two ruby blades.

A third woman, oddest yet, followed. This one was completely silver, soaked in pa, iridescent in night's cool light. And she bothered with no simple blade or dagger. No. This one held two blasters, one in either hand.

Krysta?

Ki had no time to ponder the meaning of the strange sights before him, as Elise had reached the Platform.

She climbed the steps slowly, and lesser priests scattered in every direction.

The *Ord'pa* trembled. His axe rattled in his hand.

Witnesses crowded back, away from the avenging spirit.

Ki stared at his beloved, and tentatively reached for her thoughts.

Shanna?

Elise's silver-framed eyes blazed as she looked at him. Her mind joined his, and the force of her rage nearly blew Ki off of his feet. Her sword still glinted above her head, and she locked her hands on its hilt.

"You—you bastard!" she roared, and brought the sword down with the force of a thousand warriors. The blade smote the chain binding Ki to the chopping block. Sparks flew, and the chain's links exploded.

The rest of Ki's chains fell to molten dust at his feet.

Below the Platform, the firehaired Lorelei let out a whoop and rattled her dual ruby blades. "Y'all want some of this? Come on!" She stamped the ground. "Who's your mama? Huh? Who's your mama now?"

Chapter 1

Fari Tul'Mar, Sailkeeper of Arda, never believed he would feel the Ardani mating fervor.

He had lived 120 stellar years. He was large and powerful even by Ardani standards, fit, battle-trained, and bloodthirsty when challenged. He guarded his brother Ki, the Sailmaster, with a ferocity akin to beasts of the woods. Fari knew the schematics of alien vessels as well as he knew the frigates and speeders in the Royal Fleet. His lawkeeper's mind stayed three steps ahead of potential adversaries and saboteurs.

He had no time for lunacy, and absolutely no time for a *shanna*, a soul's mate.

And yet, the moment Fari saw Georgia Steel swing her swords in front of the Tuscan Platform, the fires of mating madness had scorched him thoroughly. Stellar week after stellar week, he had been forced to consume calming elixirs prepared by the High Priest Akad. Without the drugs, and without satisfying his mounting desires, Fari would surely lose his mind.

On this day, one more in a long line of endless, grating days of frustration, he tamed his lust enough to fulfill his duties to Arda. Fari took these responsibilities more than seriously. He had learned at a tender age that mistakes and carelessness could cost precious lives.

The stables of Browntown, on the far side of Camford Lake, had been burned. The townspeople had called to the

Tul'Mar Clan for help and defense, and that meant the Sailkeeper's involvement. He had made the journey by Chimera, without hesitation or delay.

As Fari stood in Browntown amidst the smoking rubble, he used the full measure of his psi gift to see what might elude duller minds. Behind him, the town's meager population stood in silence as he worked.

There. Fari narrowed his eyes. Wood burned beyond char. *Accelerant.*

And there. The way the structure collapsed inward. *Accelerant spread in a careful circular pattern. This was not done in passionate rage. This was cold. Calculated.*

"A message." He stroked the stubble on his cheeks.

The smoldering ruins cast sinister shadows on the scarred ground.

No Chimeras had died. They had been stolen.

Fari strode across the ashen boards to get a view from the back. Almost immediately, he caught an irregularity in the nearby dirt—and an all-too-familiar object.

"*Knador!*" Arda's worst curse left Fari's lips even as he knelt to grab the rare black falcon feather. Grinding his teeth, he crushed the plume in his fist.

Darkyn Weil and the Outlanders. And they had left him a message, neatly carved in the dried, flaking earth.

The end of time is coming. You must prepare.

Fari kicked dirt over the irritating words and crammed the broken feather in his pocket. No need to distress the citizens. At least not yet.

When he turned to explore the barn once more, Fari was taken aback by the grim, resolute expressions of the townspeople. They eyed the ground where he stood, and then glanced at the feather poking from his pocket.

He sighed.

There were no secrets here.

Serious trouble was afoot, and Arda's gentle folk — the very souls who would be counting on the might of Tul'Mar to defend them — already knew.

* * * * *

Fari rode Tor, his blue Chimera stallion, toward Camford at a dead gallop. His black hair whipped his shoulders, and his black breeches and tunic flapped in the wind. As the road wound back to the castle, grain fields, grassy plains, and thick clumps of forest flew by.

Old lore held that the *Lorelei*, wild women who protected the Tul'Mar line, once lived among those ancient trees — but the *Lorelei* were phantoms no more.

Legend had come to life in the recent Battle of Camford, after a brutal speeder crash. Fari's much-adored sister Krysta had been exposed to too much *pa*, the living substance of the universe. Her hair had turned shimmering silver, like *pa* itself. Elise Tul'Mar, Fari's sister-by-marriage, also received a full-body *pa* mark in that crash, as did her cousin Georgia Steel.

Georgia. My Georgia.

Fari's eyes narrowed. His cock hardened, and a wave of madness swept his soul. If he did not put rein to his thoughts, he would be forced to drink more of the elixir in his pocket.

Georgia. His *shanna*. Even a mental image of his destined mate could instantly push him toward insanity. Fari pictured Georgia's fiery hair and shapely body. Her smooth, freckled skin called to him, as did her tempting vine-like *pa* mark. And yet she rejected him at every turn.

His fists tightened in Tor's flowing mane.

The situation was unacceptable. Surely the crazed half-Earthling half-Ardani female would soon see reason and accept him, as she should have done the first moment they met.

One day, I will ride you, Georgia. As surely as I ride this splendid beast.

That thought was enough to necessitate a swig of calming liquid.

Fari felt his tongue burn as he tasted the hateful fluid. Beneath him, Tor snorted and sang as if to bring his master's concentration back to the task at hand.

Chimera and rider thundered beneath azure skies and the bright light of big sun and little sister, Arda's daystars. Fari felt the drive of purpose clearing his fogged mind. Gradually, his intense desire abated.

He had other urgent matters to attend after the morning's investigation. After nearly one hundred and twenty-five stellar years of tenuous peace, the only opposition faction within the Tul'Mar realm was suddenly discontent.

Why would Darkyn Weil and his Outlander fools start trouble now?

The Outlanders had troubled Arda's main society since the first recorded times. They had always lived separately and secretly in tribal groups, refusing trade and interaction, waiting for *Ma'ord'pa*. The end of life. The end of time. The doom of Ardani civilization.

Tanna Kon'pa. That's what they called themselves. "The People."

As if no other people existed.

Outlanders considered themselves guardians of the ancient wisdoms and the ancient ways. Generation after generation of Outlander children had been raised to believe that one day, they would be the only hope for Arda's survival.

Which was, of course, ridiculous.

"The People" were not even telepathic. They had no *pa* mark, and thus, no direct connection to the living matter of the universe.

Suspicious bastards. Fari swore silently as the Tul'Mar family castle came into view. *Prepare for the end of time. The end is near — always the same foolish message. Arda should have blown itself to bits long ago, if Outlander propaganda were the least bit accurate.*

At the moment, though, Darkyn Weil's timing was abysmal.

Ki Tul'Mar had taken the Ardani Fleet on patrol to ward off another incursion from OrTa. Lord Gith had been defeated in the Battle of Camford a few stellar months ago, but the stinking lizard had not been destroyed. As long the slaver lived, he would try to reclaim the woman he believed to be his property: Ki's *shanna* Elise.

Fari snarled.

That would never happen. Ki would die before surrendering Elise, and Fari would die with him. As was Ardani custom, Fari had sometimes joined Ki and Elise for long sessions of sensuous lovemaking. Elise was a warm and caring woman, a golden-haired blessing from the gods. She would never *ever* become an OrTan pleasure slave.

Elise was nearing delivery of Ki's firstborn, and the babe would be heir to Camford's legacy. In Ki's absence, Fari was responsible for Elise's safety—and the safety of petulant, maddening Georgia.

Fari reined Tor at Camford's massive gates. *Georgia. My shanna. Will you forever reject me?*

As he entered the grounds, his pa mark, the shape of a great bird in flight covering his broad chest and sides, burned with Georgia's nearness.

"Where is she?" he murmured, fumbling for the elixir even as his cock responded to her proximity.

There. In front of the stables.

Georgia's hips swayed as she walked, leading her yellow Chimera. Krysta was with her. The two women had been for a morning ride.

"And probably a morning fuck," Fari grumbled to himself, borrowing the Earth word for sex. He liked its harsh, intense sound. The image of Krysta making love to his *shanna* didn't anger him, except for the fact that he had been left out. It was commonplace for Ardani to share their mates with first-degree, same generation relatives.

Exercising great force of will, Fari did not grab his rigid cock and stroke himself to relief. He fancied he could smell Georgia's light scent of wild berries and spring. Feel the brush of her skin against his throbbing pa mark.

Tor nuzzled Fari's neck and hummed.

"I have no time for this," Fari agreed. "I need to go to the war room and contact Ki. This Outlander problem…"

His words trailed off as Georgia entered the stables.

Will they fuck again, Georgia and Krysta? If I know my sister…

His cock throbbed hard against his belly.

Perhaps he could spare a few minutes to visit with his mate-to-be. If they could have a positive conversation, just one reasonable interaction, maybe he would be on the road to persuading Georgia to give him a chance.

Especially if Krysta had her primed for true satisfaction.

Grinning, Fari headed for the barn.

Chapter 2

Georgia Steel whistled quietly as she entered Camford's massive stables leading Lia, her Chimera. Krysta Tul'Mar walked just ahead with her sleek purple Chimera filly.

The barn's cool shade felt soothing to Georgia's lightly burned skin. Akad's lotions took the bite out of Arda's dual suns, but it would be a while before she could tolerate the extra-hot morning light. Or the multitude of extra-hot eager gazes from warriors and civilians alike.

Ardani citizens gawked at Georgia wherever she went, and an endless line of fascinated suitors vied for her attention. Ardani warriors. Sex gods of unimaginable proportions. And they were each dying to touch one of the *Lorelei*.

"Mythical guardian of Arda's royal family" had never been on Georgia's career list, but she got the job thanks to her best friend and distant cousin Elise. Ki, Elise's new alien husband, was a cross between a king, a sea admiral, and Captain Kirk. He was pretty cute, too.

In fact, "hunk" would describe most Ardani males. Georgia wanted to paint them all—vivid oils, bright acrylics—maybe even the occasional watercolor. Her artist's eye was certainly getting its fill of perfect male models.

Elise had rescued Georgia from the drudgery of Earth's pathetic breeding stock—even if she had nearly gotten them killed in a war between Arda's fleet of star frigates and a bunch of OrTan slaver skulls. That freaky Lord Gith got his scaly butt kicked when he tried to take Elise away from Ki, though. That was certainly worth the danger.

Georgia smiled. Since the big battle, she had been busy filling canvases with images of her new world, dodging panting warriors, spoiling Elise because she was pregnant, taking lessons with the priest Akad to learn to control her psychic energies — and experimenting with sex, sex, sex. Ki's sister Krysta had been her willing subject.

Pretty soon, she planned to bed one of the mountainous soldiers in abundance at Camford.

Ki's brother Fari, the Sailkeeper of Arda, would definitely volunteer, but Georgia found herself afraid of the hulking, brooding Fleet security officer. He was nearly seven feet tall and tended to act either totally arrogant or slightly insane in her presence — which was cause enough to feel uncomfortable around him. And yet, there were other reasons.

Fari Tul'Mar wanted to marry her, and Georgia was definitely *not* the marrying type. She had a planet full of perfect specimens to sample before she thought about settling down. And besides, while Elise had her three rules about trust and love, Georgia had just one: fuck 'em and leave 'em. No muss, no fuss. Sex was always better that way.

No doubt Fari didn't agree with that line of thinking. With his devastating good looks and swagger — he'd just assume she'd be his for the taking, and keeping, if he wanted. He'd be just like all the jocks and sun-worshippers back in high school. The guys who thought they were God's gift. The guys Georgia didn't want to think about ever again. Just the sight of him brought up old pains. Ancient fears Georgia battled with her sharp tongue and bright paints.

The Sailkeeper of Arda was hot, no question. He'd make an outstanding model, and he'd probably be a great fuck.

But Georgia didn't plan to go there.

Too risky. Too scary.

Krysta Tul'Mar, on the other hand, was tall and a little arrogant herself, but more normal. Most of the time, she didn't scare Georgia at all. This morning, Krysta had been giddy and mysterious on their ride. She seemed to be...well, up to something.

Georgia itched to find out what that might be.

When they reached the back of the stables, they eased their Chimeras into clean, well-stocked stalls. Then, Krysta turned to Georgia and grinned. "Take off your clothes."

"What?" Georgia felt a thrill. Her already pink skin turned a deep shade of red.

"Trust me," Krysta murmured. She leaned forward and gave Georgia a gentle kiss on the cheek.

And so, feeling a flush of excitement, Georgia Steel stripped naked in the far corner of the barn's large entry room. It didn't bother her that a few stable hands wandered nearby. Nakedness was nothing unusual on Arda. No one even glanced in her direction.

Georgia's auburn hair tumbled down her freckled chest, blending with the new silver tattoos all over her skin. Her *pa* wound like wild honeysuckle around her hips and breasts, and the strange substance increased her connection to herself, to Arda, and to everyone she cared about—like Elise. Like the striking woman who stood before her, dressed only in tight leather-like breeches.

Krysta gave her a sultry, teasing smile.

"Okay, I'm at your mercy." Georgia felt her nipples harden. God, she was already wet and aching. "What are you up to?"

"I have something to show you." Krysta's silvery hair shimmered in the filtered stable light, cascading over her golden shoulders and covering parts of her own *pa* pattern of soft cherry blossoms. Her full breasts tempted Georgia, but Krysta hadn't let her do more than a few touches during their morning ride.

Behind them, their Chimeras enjoyed a snack of sweetgrain. Their nickering sounded like soft music, reinforcing Georgia's belief that the creatures were at least part unicorn. Part giraffe, part horse—something utterly different than anything she had seen on Earth.

But then, so was the dark-haired, night-eyed Krysta, who was pushing a set of buttons on the stable wall.

A panel slid open, and Krysta disappeared from view.

Welcome to Arda. Part Camelot, part Star Trek.

Smiling, Georgia followed.

The room she stepped into was small but bright, lit by skylights and candles. A bed took up the far wall, and several contraptions made the floor an obstacle course. Two of the hurdles looked like waist-high saddles, almost touching at the pommels, with thick, tempting penises growing out of the centers.

Georgia raised an eyebrow and glanced at Krysta. "Is this another lesson in how sexually deprived I've been on Earth?"

"Mmm-hmm. Come here." Krysta beckoned, and Georgia joined her in front of the saddles.

In the stellar weeks that Georgia had been on Arda, Krysta's embrace had become familiar—but no less exciting. Her kisses were sweet and deep, comforting and thrilling at the same time. Georgia loved the feel of Krysta's breasts rubbing against her skin, and the softness of Krysta's tongue tracing her lips. Still, Georgia missed the feel of a hot cock, and a man's muscles flexing beneath her hands.

A man like the Sailkeeper.

For the briefest of moments, Georgia imagined Fari's powerful embrace. What would his lips feel like, claiming hers? How would he taste?

Enough! Damn. I'm losing it.

She jerked her attention back to reality and purred as Krysta stroked the small of her back with nimble fingers. Krysta leaned down. Their taut nipples met, and their *pa* marks touched.

Georgia gasped at the electric tingle, and took another deep breath of Krysta's perfume of mint and fresh air. Before she could get her bearings, Krysta moved her hand between Georgia's legs and whispered, "Sweet and wet. Your quim always feels so warm."

Georgia moaned as Krysta rubbed her clit, finding the hot spot instantly. "Good. Right there. You get it every time."

"I try." Krysta nibbled at Georgia's lip, increasing the speed and pressure of her strokes.

Closing her eyes, Georgia rocked against Krysta's hand. "Faster. Faster!"

Krysta obliged, rubbing hard and pulling Georgia against her silken skin until Georgia shook and groaned with her climax.

Instead of laying Georgia down for more, Krysta pushed her backwards, toward one of the penis-saddles. "Sit on the *kala* now."

Georgia hesitated, but Krysta smiled. "Trust me. Sit."

Knees shaking from her orgasm, Georgia lowered herself, expecting the shock of penetration. Instead, the penis-like protrusion slipped inside her as if it were no larger than a finger.

For a moment, nothing happened.

And then the protrusion expanded.

And expanded.

And kept expanding, until Georgia couldn't stand another millimeter.

"God, this feels so good. Like a custom-designed dildo." Georgia let out a long moan and wiggled on the saddle. It was warm against her backside, and the form-fitting penis moved with her. Teasing. Almost thrusting.

Krysta settled on the other saddle, close enough to kiss if Georgia leaned forward. She didn't. The feel of the expanding penis was too intense. Krysta's satisfied expression told Georgia that her pussy had been filled to capacity, too.

"Use your thoughts," Krysta said as she rocked slowly, back and forth. "Guide the *kala*. It will follow your psi-commands."

Georgia nodded, unable to speak as she willed her saddle to move in the way she wanted.

The custom-penis thrust deep inside her slit—but not too deep. "Oh, damn." She gripped the saddle's edge, grinding herself on it as hard as she could.

"Good, yes?" Krysta rocked more forcefully. She reached out and grasped the ends of Georgia's nipples and rolled them between her fingers.

Georgia cried out and arched against her saddle. *Harder*, she insisted, and the saddle bucked. *Harder!*

Krysta must have been giving similar orders to her *kala*, because it rammed up and back, drawing deep moans of pleasure. Georgia turned loose her saddle and captured Krysta's nipples, enjoying the fierce look of pleasure on Krysta's face as she squeezed.

A strange sensation pierced Georgia's shoulder blades. She had the feeling someone other than Krysta was watching. Instead of horrifying her, the feeling doubled Georgia's excitement. Tension built in her belly as she rode her saddle and kneaded Krysta's breasts. Krysta pinched back with a vengeance, and Georgia groaned.

"Hope you like what you're seeing," she managed to gasp for the benefit of their secret admirer.

Krysta laughed and tweaked Georgia's nipples harder.

Like a hot wave, sensation rose and rose until Georgia exploded with a loud yell.

Krysta came almost at the same moment. She let Georgia's nipples go and grabbed her saddle, undulating as the *kalas* eased them down with slower and more gentle thrusts.

That "someone's watching" sensation stopped suddenly, and Georgia turned toward the door.

It was closed. No one was there.

"Oooh. A shy one." She wiggled in spite of herself. The *kala* responded with a soft nudge inside her, and the aftershock was delicious. "I need to find him. Shy men are tons of fun."

"That man might surprise you," Krysta said. She looked uncomfortable.

Georgia felt too relaxed to let the comment bother her. After a few seconds of inactivity, she felt the protrusion shrink inside her, and she eased off of it without difficulty. "That was wild. Do you have—um, more unbelievably wonderful sex toys?"

Krysta's dark eyes twinkled. "I think you would be served better by an unbelievably wonderful warrior. My brother for example. "

Georgia climbed off the *kala*. "He's spooky, Krysta."

"Fari is intense." Krysta slid off her saddle. "But he is the Sailkeeper—like one of your Earth policemen. It is his job to be alert for treachery, to protect the Sailmaster and the fleet. Besides, you are his soul's mate. When he nears you, his senses overwhelm him."

Georgia suddenly wished for her clothes, but they were in the outer room. "Soul's mate. How can he know that?"

"Has Akad failed to explain psi-connections in your lessons?" Krysta's tone reflected concern.

Georgia sighed and did her best to shield her thoughts. Of course Akad had explained psi-connections, and the finding and knowing of one's soul's mate. In great detail. Daily. Georgia just hadn't wanted to listen.

She started for the door of the pleasure room.

Fuck 'em and leave 'em. No muss, no fuss. After growing up an orphan, and after what happened in high school— soul's mate? No thank you.

Other than Elise, Georgia had never given her heart or trust to anyone, and she couldn't imagine giving herself to Fari Tul'Mar in any sense of the word.

Oh, yes I can. That's why he scares me so much. God. I need to shut up, and I don't need to think about Fari.

Georgia shivered, and Krysta put an arm around her shoulders as they stepped back into the main area.

"I did not mean to distress you, Sister," Krysta said softly. "It seems some shadow covers your heart."

The warmth of Krysta's embrace chased back Georgia's cold thoughts. "No big deal. Really. But as for Fari, I don't know *what* to do about him."

"Take your time, if time is what you need." Krysta kissed Georgia gently. "Fari will wait forever, if necessary."

"I hope such torture will not be my fate." Fari Tul'Mar's resonant voice flooded Georgia's senses. Her heart skipped and shuddered. She wheeled around to find the Sailkeeper of Arda leaning against the door frame.

Fari was dressed in his tight black breeches and tunic. The laces were open, showing the wings of his *pa* mark, and his barbed blade hung in a scabbard at his side. His long hair was loose about his shoulders, and he had a hint of beard on his chin and cheeks. Just enough to look completely sexy—and insufferably haughty.

Truth gripped Georgia like a vise. "It was you watching us."

Fari shrugged. "You did not mind at the time."

"I didn't know who it was!" Anger heated Georgia's insides. She turned on Krysta. "But *you* did."

Krysta held up her hands, pleading. "I was having an orgasm. It was impossible to stop."

Georgia wanted to believe her, but the damage had been done, at least for the moment. She covered herself as best she could before facing Fari again.

He stepped in front of her, cutting off the route to her clothes.

"Please get out of my way," Georgia said, irritated at the squeaky pitch of her voice. "I need to get dressed."

For a moment, Fari didn't move. A smile played at his full lips, and Georgia's cheeks flushed. She wanted to lunge forward and smack him, but she would have to uncover herself to do that—and damned if she'd give him that kind of pleasure again.

"Get the hell out of my way," she repeated through clenched teeth.

Again, Fari hesitated, but before Georgia completely lost her temper, he gave her a flourishing bow and stepped aside.

She brushed past him, and his thoughts trickled into her mind.

You are so beautiful. If you would give me but a chance, I could please you like no other…

Georgia hesitated. She looked back, directly into Fari's fathomless black eyes. Her *pa* mark crackled and snapped, and her body's response was beyond denying. For a moment, she allowed him to stay in her brain. She let herself imagine his arms around her. His mouth covering hers. His hard cock pressed against her aching pussy.

Her very essence ached for his touch. She felt like she was on a roller coaster, plunging down and down. There was something about this man. Something special.

Damn him to fifty hells!

Fari groaned and stepped toward her.

Fear pierced Georgia's reverie, followed by a wave of rage. The barn's walls seemed to close in on her, and her breath left in a rush. Fari was too close. Even Krysta was too close. The whole place felt like a closet.

A storage closet. Papers, stacked to the ceiling. Boxes everywhere.

"No!" Georgia stumbled backward. Her heart raced. *Elise. Where's Elise? I need Elise.*

"What is wrong, Sister?" Krysta extended a hand.

So did Fari. Concern erased the hard lines of his face, giving him a softer, tender look.

Georgia couldn't process any of it. She couldn't breathe.

"Stay away from me!" she shouted as she grabbed her clothes and ran. "Leave me alone!"

Chapter 3

Fari Tul'Mar's head spun with the force of his rage. He didn't chase Georgia because he understood her reticence after the broadcast of her dark memories.

And someday, somehow, the bastard responsible for her terror would face justice at the Sailkeeper's hands.

Fari's gut ached as he watched his *shanna* flee the barn because long ago, a man had injured her body and spirit. Now, males and sex — it was all a game to her. She trusted her heart to no one save Elise.

Georgia's sweet scent of wild berries lingered in the air as if to torment him.

Krysta grabbed his elbow. "If you would cease acting like an arrogant fergilla, perhaps she would cease running from you."

"Leave me be." Fari doubled his fists. Images of torturing the scum who hurt Georgia almost overtook him. "She has wounds of the heart. I did not know until this moment."

"Because you never looked." Krysta slipped around him and picked up her shirt. "We all have secrets, Fari. Old hurts and old shames — as you well know. Still — I, I, I. That is all I hear from you. Even now, you think of maiming some attacker from Georgia's past instead of soothing her fears *today*. If you keep this up, she will choose a mate at the Festival of Seasons just to be rid of you."

"Festival of Seasons. Hmph. Only fools would submit themselves to such humiliation." And yet pain pierced Fari's head like a Chimera had kicked him between the eyes. The thought of Georgia mating with another man—that would not happen. No. Murderous was too mild a word for Fari's feelings on that subject.

Steady. Do not let the mating fervor overtake you again.

He chewed the inside of his cheek rather than fire an angry speech at his sister—though Krysta could hold her own in a war of words. In any war, for that matter.

"Here." He extracted the crushed falcon feather from his pocket and thrust it at her. "Contact Ki. Tell him the Outlanders burned the Browntown stables."

"What?" Krysta snatched the evidence and stared at it. "But—why?"

Fari conveyed his findings from the morning's investigation in terse phrases, fighting to keep his thoughts off Georgia. "I suspect some celestial portent of doom has set them off again."

"'The end of time is coming.'" Krysta nodded. "Do you think—"

"Please. Just contact Ki." Fari rubbed the sides of his aching head. "I cannot discuss this now."

Krysta offered no argument, and wordless in his disgrace, Fari stalked down the long corridor and left the barn.

I am a fool. Impulsive, as always. Will I forever miss what is vital? Camford's stone walls loomed before him. He hurried up the main steps to the massive wooden doors. *From this point forward, I will take more care with my* shanna. *I will apologize for my past insensitivity, and then I will join Krysta in the war room to deal with the Outlanders.*

His lip curled. "And when we claim victory, I will turn my attentions to the fergilla who hurt my beloved."

Even without a psi-touch, Fari knew where Georgia had gone. To Ki's bedchamber. To Elise. She was seeking comfort from her sister-cousin—the comfort Fari fiercely wished she would allow him to offer.

In typical Sailkeeper fashion, he strode straight toward his target. His mind churned on what he would say and the tone he should choose. He knew more nervousness than he had ever known, which angered him at both the circumstance and himself.

Not until Fari stood outside the bedchamber door did he realize he was courting disaster. His emotions howled like a fall storm. His body tensed as though he stood on the razor-edge of a precipice.

If he walked in that room in his current state, he would make an overbearing fool of himself again.

Growling like a crazed game cat, Fari forced himself to turn away. Akad's potion tasted bitter indeed as he swallowed a good-sized gulp. It hit him in seconds, and he staggered against the wall to keep from falling.

For long stellar minutes, he stood facing the wall, bracing himself with both hands on the cold stone. He let his head droop, waiting for the elixir's effects to settle.

Georgia is on the other side of this rock, his fevered brain informed him.

And he could see her in his mind, stretched across the big curtained bed. She lay with her head in Elise's lap, and Elise stroked her hair tenderly.

Fari's fantasies swirled, and he fancied his *shanna* rolling to her back. Her clothes melted away, and he saw her as he did in the barn. Naked and aroused. Her red locks swirled about her freckled shoulders, and between her legs—a matching blaze. Moisture glistened on the fiery hair.

A groan echoed through the hallway, and Fari realized it came from his own throat. His cock pulsed and swelled, overriding Akad's medicine. He had to find relief before his body exploded.

Fari's first thought was to bash his head against the rocks until he fell unconscious. Perhaps then he would know respite from this burning desire. Akad needed to brew something stronger before the unsatisfied mating fervor killed him outright. Had any warrior waited so long—or done so poorly in winning his destined mate?

I am a bigger fool than I thought.

A wave of dizziness drove Fari to his knees. He struggled not to vomit. Like drums, his blood thrummed in his ears. Camford's air felt thick and heavy. He could barely force it into his lungs.

What was happening?

Had he been poisoned?

He swayed, almost pitched onto the marble floor—and then strong hands gripped his shoulder, his arm. And softer hands, on his other arm. Camford spun around him in a swirl of colors. Someone was helping him up, urging him to walk.

He staggered.

A tall figure caught him. Krysta, by the feel of fergilla hide beneath his shaking hands. His sister and her bodysuits.

Fari closed his eyes. In seconds, he was eased into a bed.

...Took too much of the elixir... Akad's voice roused him some time later. Fari struggled to make sense of the words.

He was trying to control the fervor... Krysta? Elise?

The light scent of berries tickled Fari's nose, and his soul ached. Fari frowned. The universe was cursing him. He would die without knowing his *shanna*, and it would be his own fault.

He looks so bad. The new voice sliced through his confusion. *Is this my fault?*

"No!" Fari barked. He would not have Georgia blaming herself for his foolishness. Somehow, he forced his eyes open. His *shanna* was standing beside him, looking distraught. The expression pained him to no end.

Using all of his strength, Fari reached for her.

Georgia took his hand.

"I am s-sorry," he managed before darkness swept him away.

Chapter 4

Shock stabbed Georgia like cold knives. Fari's massive hand lay limp in hers, and she didn't want to let him go.

"Is this a joke?" she whispered.

"No." Akad pushed his brown hair behind his ears, revealing the swirls of *pa* on his cheeks. The handsome priest looked sad and worried as he tended the Sailkeeper of Arda with infinite tenderness. The warrior giant seemed near death — and from what Georgia could tell, Fari was dying of mating fervor. Or rather, prolonged exposure to the elixir Akad had given him to control the related madness.

He was dying because she wouldn't fuck him.

Oh, great.

"He's not dying," Elise assured her. "He's taken a toxic amount of elixir. Akad can fix things."

Georgia glanced at her cousin. Elise's cheeks were plump and rosy from her late-stage pregnancy. She wore one of her husband's tunics, which fit her like a dress. Her golden hair shimmered, as did the flames of *pa* covering her skin. Georgia had never seen Elise healthier, or happier.

Fari, in contrast, lay pale on Ki's bed like a patient awaiting surgery. Akad had removed Fari's shirt, and the Sailkeeper's muscled chest looked iron-hard and tempting. The wings of his *pa* mark seemed dim and sallow, which unnerved Georgia even more than the obvious hard-on straining at the black fabric of Fari's tight breeches.

"I don't want him," she muttered to herself. "I don't want him. I don't."

But the simple sensation of his hand in hers made her heart beat faster. His chiseled body, his huge, stiff cock—all of him made her pussy ache. Could this man give her as much happiness as Ki had given Elise? Sweat broke out on Georgia's forehead.

Shielding her thoughts, she cursed herself. She'd fucked dozens of guys. One night stands, one week stands. Hell, she'd even kept a few of them for a month or more. Cops, sailors, grocery clerks, panty-waste bosses—it never mattered much to her as long as they were good looking and had the proper equipment. Why couldn't she fuck this guy once and have done with it?

No muss, no fuss. Who cares if he wants to marry me? I don't have to say yes. It certainly wouldn't be a hardship to sleep with this guy. I mean, look at him. He's beautiful. He's perfect.

The reality of Fari's suffering and how he had controlled his desires to accommodate her made Georgia think twice about his arrogance. If an Earth man had wanted her so much it hurt, he likely would have taken what he desired and found a way to blame her for it later.

Like Chuck Sampson did.

The shadow of Georgia's high school nightmare chilled her, and Fari's grip on her hand tightened.

Never again, beloved. His voice whispered in her mind, as gentle as a light kiss. *I will kill any man who even thinks of hurting you.*

Georgia gasped, but she kept her death-hold on Fari's hand. She knew she must have broadcast the reason for her panic in the barn. And now, this man knew her worst secret. He was half-dead, and he chose to spend his energy comforting her.

She chanced another look at him. Fari's ink-black eyes were partially open and trained on her. She saw no trickery or deceit.

Only raw desire. And something else. Affection? Caring?

Georgia's heart rate doubled, but she still didn't let him go. Her gaze swept his full, muscled length, and her body stirred. The *pa* on her skin heated rapidly, and her pussy throbbed.

What would it hurt, to fuck him once and see what it felt like?

Elise said he was a fantastic lover, even if she'd never felt that incredible cock inside her pussy. That kind of contact was for Ki alone—but Elise could vouch for Fari's oral and back-door talents, not to mention his raw sensuality. She said he was honest, gentle, and straightforward.

Intense.

Yes. Those eyes are beyond intense.

Fari managed a slightly delirious smile.

"Okay, enough." Georgia let go of Fari's hand and turned to Akad. "Work your magic, then take him to my room."

Akad's gasp was audible. So was Krysta's sharp intake of breath.

Elise's expression shifted from thrilled to worried and back to thrilled again. She threw her arms around Georgia.

"Are you sure? It's such a big step! Marriage, commitment—"

"Whoa." Georgia pushed her cousin back. "I didn't say anything about marriage. This is about sex. Fucking. Nothing less, nothing more. Got me?"

"But—" Elise, Akad, and Krysta began before Fari interrupted them with a cough.

"My *shanna's* terms are acceptable to me." He struggled to prop himself up on his elbows. "If I cannot please her or win her heart, she has no obligation to me."

Krysta paled. "You would release her? Brother! Do not be foolish."

"Is somebody going to behead you, Fari?" Elise's question came out in a rush. "If there's some freaky Ardani ritual involved in this, you'd best tell us now or I'll kill you myself."

"There is not." Akad answered evenly and honestly, as always. "Fari is Sailkeeper, not Sailmaster. He would not lose his position or his life if Georgia refused him."

Already, Georgia had learned enough of Arda's fine arts of omission to ask, "What *would* he lose?"

Akad gave her a perplexed shrug. "I do not know. We have never faced such a situation."

"In the history of Arda, no woman has refused her soul's mate?" Georgia's stomach twisted.

"Not ever." Krysta folded her arms and gazed at her brother. "Soul's mates know each other at a spirit-level. They have no reason to refuse the natural call to mating."

"Stop this." Fari sounded stronger, but when he tried to sit up, he sagged back to the pillows.

Akad bent to check his pulse, but Fari pushed the priest away.

"I do not care what has or has not happened in our history." His words sounded much stronger than he looked. "Georgia made a request of me, and I granted it with a glad heart. The rest is for us to decide. Alone."

With that, he locked gazes with Georgia again.

Damn. The man can barely move, and he's more sexy than any guy I've fucked. The knots in Georgia's stomach became tight macramé. Elise's smile and Krysta's wide-eyed worry annoyed her. Even the priest's gentle smile made Georgia want to smack something. With a snort, she smoothed her tunic and loose riding pants. The fabric stroked her skin like the gentle touch of a hundred fingers.

"When he's better, bring him to my room." Georgia managed to keep her voice from trembling. "I'll be waiting."

Akad leaned toward her and handed her a small brown vial. "We have discussed this."

Georgia nodded. Before anyone could say another word, she pocketed the bottle of relaxing elixir and made a dignified exit from Ki and Elise's quarters.

When she reached the hall and shut the door behind her, she had a powerful urge to run like hell and never look back. Her bedchamber seemed hundreds of miles away, and way too close.

If I run, he's too weak to catch me…at least for now.

And then an idea occurred to her.

"He can't catch me in his condition, but I could catch him." Georgia glanced back at the chamber door. A commotion was rising inside, and she knew it was Fari, forcing everyone to hurry.

"Bring it on, big man." Georgia grinned as she started for her room. "We'll see who *your* mama is. Yeah."

Chapter 5

Fari woke slowly, as if from a long, battle-earned sleep.

What happened? I was in the stables, and — and I cannot remember.

He shook his head to clear the brain-fog. Even his psi-senses felt dull. The ache in his muscles was tolerable, but annoying. As his thoughts sharpened, his investigative instincts took over.

He was naked, lying atop a bed with soft sheets and many pillows. A four-poster, but not the bed in Ki's chamber. All around the room stood easels with canvases in various states of finish. There, a striking sunrise, with big sun and little sister glowing over Camford's towers. Beside that, Camford Lake, complete with gentle, sparkling waves. A few unfinished nudes — one male, one female.

Covered pallets rested in the windowsills, and brushes soaked in jars on every tabletop. An artist lived in this room, but who?

The intricate carvings on the bedposts, walls, and ceilings told Fari he was deep inside Camford, and the slant of light through the large windows suggested the west wing.

Where Georgia Steel had been staying.

The moment his *shanna's* name entered Fari's mind, his senses woke. He remembered what occurred in Elise and Ki's room, and he could smell wild berries, like the first breezes of spring.

Fiery energy crackled along his *pa* mark. Georgia was near him.

Heat welled in Fari's gut, and his cock responded.

He had to find her and talk to her. He needed to touch her. But first, Akad's potion, so he wouldn't be a clumsy, insane fool.

Fari reached for his pocket—but his arm wouldn't move. At that moment, he realized he was bound to the bed by his ankles and wrists.

"What is this?" He growled, struggling against his tethers.

"Don't worry," a feminine voice purred. "I won't hurt you."

"*Shanna.*" Fari turned his head to the left.

Georgia stood between the bed and one of the floor-to-ceiling windows wearing nothing but a taunting smile. Sunslight spilled through her auburn hair and bathed her creamy, freckled skin in bright yellow heat. Her dark nipples beaded as he stared. She ran her hands over her hips, dangerously near the red curls between her legs, and Fari groaned.

His brain threatened to short-circuit. He had wild fantasies of breaking his bonds, throwing her to the bed, and fucking her like an animal.

Calm, he told himself. *Gentle.*

"Calm and gentle for now," she murmured, reading his thoughts. "I may want it wild later."

Fari pulled against his cloth shackles as she took a teasing step toward him. He tried to assent, but only managed a delirious grunt.

"I'm going to try you and see how I like you." Georgia moved slowly, almost as if she were dancing.

Fari's cock throbbed. The fire in his body and mind nearly blinded him, but he kept his eyes focused on the vision approaching him.

Georgia smiled. She was close enough now to trail one finger down his shoulder. The feel of her flesh against his made him groan again.

"Do you like that idea?" Georgia's finger traveled across his chest, nearly touching the wings of Fari's *pa* mark.

Fari felt like a space frigate's ion engine strapped to a child's skysailer. Any second, he would explode and burn the works to cinders. Still, he forced his throat and mouth to cooperate, at least long enough to bark, "Yes."

"'Here's the deal." Georgia sat on the bed beside him, but kept her touch to the single finger on his hip, inching slowly toward his cock. "We do this my way. You don't try anything I'm not ready for."

Biting the inside of his cheek, Fari nodded.

"We're not married. We're not even committed. I just want to fuck you, and you will *not* get me pregnant. Are we clear?"

Fari managed another nod.

Georgia fell silent, but continued her sensual massage, now with her entire hand on his thigh. She squeezed and prodded the muscle in his upper leg, then his calf. And then she started back up again.

Dizzy, fighting instinct and primal drive, Fari clenched his fists. He heard the soft tear of fabric and quickly willed his bonds to hold. If he tore himself free, Georgia might stop.

Oblivious to the noise, or perhaps unable to hear it over Fari's labored breathing, Georgia toyed with the hair around his cock. She almost touched the tender sac beneath—and then moved on, toward the base of his *pa* mark, which surrounded his groin. He tensed.

"If I touch this while you're so...aroused...will it hurt?" Georgia's soft voice made the ache in Fari's soul deeper.

He had to have this woman *now. Now!*

Battling a wave of raging desire, he shook his head. "It will be intensely pleasurable. For both of us."

Georgia gazed into his eyes for a long moment.

Fari felt his heart swell. He wanted to hold her, to cradle her—but all in good time, when she was ready.

With a sigh, she ran her hand across his *pa*.

Hot shocks traveled Fari's body. His cock jerked, and he nearly came from the electric pleasure.

Georgia gasped and closed her eyes. Her own *pa* crackled audibly, and Fari felt her thoughts wrap around his. He could feel what she felt, and his ferocious want doubled. His *shanna's* clit was aching. The intensity of her desire surprised her. Pleased her. And frightened her.

Do not fear me, beloved. Fari shook from his efforts not to tear free from the bed. *I will never harm you. I will protect you, with my very life.*

"I want to believe you," she whispered. Her hand moved from his *pa* to his cock, drawing a growl of need from his very depths. "You're so big. So hard."

Up and down went her skilled hand. Her artist's hand.

Every muscle in Fari's body roared. The pressure, the silk of her skin on his—the sensation was perfect.

When she opened her fathomless green eyes, he could see appreciation. Her pleasure in his manhood.

"Elise told me Ardani men can come over and over again. Is that true?"

Fari ground his teeth. "Yes. Especially with the right woman's attention."

"Mmm-mmm." Georgia picked up the speed of her massage. "Let's find out if I'm the right woman."

In seconds, Fari could hold himself back no longer. He came with a gut-jarring blast, spilling his seed on Georgia's hand and chest—but she didn't stop. She kept stroking.

"Get hard again for me. Let me see."

And Fari obliged. He couldn't have refused the demand, even if he had wished to.

As Georgia pumped his swelling cock, she licked his seed from her hand. The tip of her tongue teased his hard, sensitive flesh.

You are trying to drive me to madness, he said in his calmest psi-voice.

Georgia didn't answer.

Instead, she flicked her tongue against his cock again.

Fari groaned.

"You taste good," she murmured, and then took his length in her sizzling, flower-soft mouth.

This time, Fari did rip one of his bonds as he convulsed. With sheer force of will, he left his arm still, as if he remained tied.

Georgia moved her mouth up and down his swollen shaft, sucking, then stopping to kiss and lick the tip. Her fingers cupped his sac, and he was lost.

Using all of his strength to remain motionless and keep the other bonds intact, Fari immersed himself in her sensual assault. He had enjoyed the talents of many women, but none to compare to this unpredictable firebrand.

His match. His equal. His shanna.

She sucked him hard and deep. So satisfying. Fari heard his own rumbles of pleasure as he came again.

Once more, Georgia didn't let up. She drank his seed as if it were wine, and her thoughts told him she enjoyed the warmth and taste.

Georgia's thoughts also let him know that she didn't realize the bonds on his right leg had broken. So much the better.

She halted her relentless attack and smiled at him.

Fari smiled back.

He could do this "Georgia's way" all day and all night. Forever, if necessary. Touching her, feeling her against him, knowing she was taking pleasure in his body, his presence — these things felt like rewards for his long days of pain and deprivation. If it was the last thing he ever did, Fari Tul'Mar vowed to himself, he would win this woman's trust, and her heart.

Chapter 6

Georgia sat beside Fari and kept one hand on his chest. On his *pa*. The sight of him tied up, completely at her disposal and enjoying it—what a rush. She held the image in her mind, intent on painting it later.

Not that she wanted him to know that.

Georgia's paintings were too close to her heart to discuss, and she rarely shared them or showed them to others, even Elise. Some parts of her mind and heart, Georgia Steel shared with no one.

And so, she battled to guard her thoughts. For some reason, Georgia didn't want Fari to know how attractive she found him.

At first it had been an eye-candy thing. A cheap thrill. The thought of alien sex with a warrior god. But now, Georgia was feeling something else. Something warmer, and infinitely more frightening.

She licked her lips.

Damn, but his come tasted good. Sweet and salt mixed, like a rich, warm cream. And the feel of his cock in her mouth, how the thick length had filled her hand—she was too wet for words. Her pussy ached. Her nipples twinged for attention. She felt linked to this man, connected at some basic level.

She had never wanted to be fucked so badly in her entire life.

What *was* it about Fari Tul'Mar?

Okay, so his body was a painter's dream. He had dark eyes she could swim in for days. Even the stubble on his chin was sexy as hell. And yet, it was more than that. The fire she felt was too deep for simple attraction.

Am I falling in love? Could this arrogant ass really *be my soul's mate?*

No. That was stupid. She didn't know enough about him to fall in love with him. So, it had to be lust.

Good. Lust was much safer.

The salty, fundamental smell of male rose like steam around Georgia. Fari's skin felt firm and taut beneath her fingers, and she dropped her defenses enough to hear his thoughts.

Beautiful...so beautiful. I will care for you always. I will please you like no man.

A wild dizziness swept over Georgia. She wanted him inside her. Had to have him—craved him.

As he watched with that intense coal-black gaze, Georgia pushed herself up and straddled his belly. He felt as firm as carved wood between her legs, yet warm and yielding.

Fari took a slow breath. His stiff cock pressed against her ass.

Georgia scooted back and rubbed against it.

"Wait, shanna." Fari stirred beneath her, straining his bonds. "You have not been prepared. Akad gave you—"

"I don't need elixir to handle you." Georgia heard the sharp, desperate edge in her own voice. "I've been playing with Krysta's toys. I'm ready."

Fari's concerned expression only increased Georgia's passion. The man was all metal and grit on the outside, but his heart seemed so soft and giving.

Before he could protest again, she pushed up on her knees and lifted herself over his cock. The blazing tip pressed against her slit.

Groaning, Georgia sank down slowly.

The sound of wet flesh slipping into wet flesh nearly made her come.

Her eyes closed of their own volition as her pussy stretched to accommodate Fari's incredible girth.

"By the stars..." Fari's guttural welcome rolled over Georgia's skin like a kiss.

And then she dropped, taking the rest of him in one daring thrust.

"Damn!" Her eyes flew open.

Fari's eyes were closed. His face was a study in ecstasy.

He felt hotter than molten silver. Harder than polished steel. Huge. Fari's cock was unbelievably big— but Georgia felt no pain. A surge of rapture, yes. Of perfect satiation and rightness. He filled her pussy to the brim.

Damn. Damn! Heat consumed Georgia as she leaned down and braced her hands against Fari's rock hard stomach and scorching *pa*. His muscles rippled as she ground herself against his hips, letting go a loud cry.

"Shanna." Fari's fervent growls sent thrills up Georgia's spine. "Fuck me. Please yourself!"

She rocked forward and back, forward and back, savoring his size, his strength as he thrust off the bed despite his bonds. Her skin burned. Every place she touched Fari burned.

"Harder." Georgia forced herself up and down, riding him like she rode Krysta's saddle in the barn. Her ass slapped against Fari's muscled thighs.

Anything for you, Fari whispered in her mind, opening his eyes and swallowing her with his tender gaze.

Life, time, the world — everything receded for Georgia. All she could see was Fari's handsome face, the way he studied her and worked to please her with every movement.

Moaning with each thrust, she tweaked her own nipples.

Fari's male approval was instantly apparent. His eyes flared, and he bucked harder against her.

"Come," he murmured. "Come for me."

I want to see your face, Georgia. I want to see your bliss.

The low thunder of Fari's voice in her thoughts and in her ears drove Georgia higher. Her head spun. She felt wide open as she neared the top. Wild. Completely free.

Need blinded her.

"Fuck me harder," she demanded. "Yes. Deep. Deep!"

Every ounce of reserve drained out of Georgia. She bounced so hard her breasts strained against her hands. She pinched her nipples and screamed as her pussy pulsed and tightened on Fari's cock.

No man had ever seen her frenzied, but Georgia didn't care. It felt so good to turn loose and fuck like there was no tomorrow.

Seconds stretched and blended as one as she panted. Sweat coated her body.

Fari's thrusts met her each time she slammed against him.

Heat flowed from Georgia's pussy, up to her belly, to her chest, to her throat, to her cheeks.

Orgasm hit her like a flash flood, washing every muscle, every fiber with delicious thrills. She shuddered and fell forward from the force, and her *pa* mark melded with Fari's.

Immediately, images spilled through Georgia's brain. She saw herself as beautiful, sexy, completely desirable and satisfying. Fari cared about her deeply. More than she understood—and yet she couldn't deny it. His feelings, his thoughts were hers for the taking.

Fari came with a reverberating groan.

Georgia felt the heat of his seed filling her as aftershocks shook her again and again.

She wanted to move, to separate their *pa* marks. The intimacy was too much.

Tears brimmed and spilled down her face.

She had to move.

But some part of her didn't want to.

"May I hold you?" Fari's gentle words rattled Georgia.

No! her mind screamed. And then, *yes.*

As Fari's firm, sculpted arms wrapped around her, Georgia realized the brawny giant had torn his cloth tethers as if they were threads. He had been free the entire time they fucked—and yet he had left her in control, to do as she pleased.

This made her cry harder.

Fari eased Georgia to her side, but kept his cock inside her pussy. He stroked her hair with his big hands, kissed her cheeks and forehead.

Beloved. Shanna. Whatever you wish. Whatever you need.

"Shut up." Georgia sobbed and snuggled closer. Fari's touch soothed her, even though she didn't want it to.

Risking a glance at his face, she found him staring at her intently. He lowered his head and gave her a slow, languid kiss.

Georgia couldn't help but respond. Her lips parted, allowing his tongue free access. He moved against her, drawing her even closer. Their *pa* mingled like their mouths, blending thought and emotion until Georgia lost track of which feelings and sensations were hers alone.

Fari rubbed and squeezed her ass. Her nipples pressed against his hard chest, and his cock swelled in her wet channel.

I want you again, but only if you desire me, Georgia.

"I desire you," she murmured, rolling against him, taking him deeper.

"Then tell me. Say it out loud." He kissed her, then drew back. "Give me permission."

Tears still streaming, Georgia ran her fingers through Fari's ebony hair. "Fuck me. That's what I want. Fuck me."

Fari moaned and gripped her ass, pulling her hard against his cock. He made no move to mount her. They stayed on their sides, undulating like matching waves.

Georgia gasped and rocked on Fari's rigid arousal. He cradled her against him, kissing her, thrusting gently. Then faster, and faster.

This time, Georgia kept her mind open to Fari. Their thoughts flowed back and forth. Desire. Heat. Passion. Georgia felt herself being fucked, and felt what Fari experienced as he fucked her.

Amazing. Mind-bending.

"You are perfect," Fari murmured in her ear. "Everything I have dreamed of."

Pressure built in Georgia's chest. Her pussy felt hot enough to catch fire. Each time her nipples moved against Fari's chest, shocks of pleasure rattled her.

She came in slow, soul-shaking tremors, each one stronger than the next, until she cried out.

Fari drank her screams with another deep, tender kiss. His orgasm matched her own as he spent himself slowly, completely inside her.

When Georgia could take no more, she pushed at Fari's chest, and he stopped.

Just like that.

She didn't even have to insist.

Carefully, Fari eased his cock out of her pussy and held her tightly.

Georgia's eyes closed. Sleep was only inches away, but she startled awake.

No! I can't do this. Fear clawed her like an angry cat. *I don't fall asleep with men I fuck. You need to leave, Fari.*

"Is that what you want, shanna? Truly?" Fari's disappointment dug at Georgia's heart.

"Yes. No. I—I don't know." She ground her teeth, feeling her panic double as Fari massaged her shoulders in a slow, sensuous rhythm—and then, for a long, blissful moment, she let herself sink into his touch. He felt so good, so steady, like a rock she could lean on. Like a man she could trust.

Not happening.

She jerked away from him. Rage flamed in Georgia's belly, and before she knew it, she had raised her fists. "Look. We made a deal. My way or no way. And I said *leave.*"

A wild look came over Fari. He opened his mouth, and Georgia tried to shield her heart. Men were all the same. Earth, Arda—it didn't matter.

Tease.

Whore.

You led me on.

This was your fault.

You asked for it.

Fari's eyes widened, and Georgia realized she had shouted her thoughts at him.

"I would never say those things," Fari said in a hoarse, wounded voice. "You confuse me with another place, another time. I—I was thinking of asking for—no it doesn't matter. I am honored that you shared yourself with me."

He was out of the bed before Georgia could react, and out of the room before she could form a coherent thought.

Wait...

But it was too late.

For such a big man, Fari Tul'Mar moved like the wind.

Chapter 7

One day, she will judge you on your own merits, with no hindrance from her past. Ki Tul'Mar's psi-voice drifted over the stellar leagues separating him from Fari. You cannot force so much as a conversation with a woman who has been forced — not without losing her trust.

Fari sat, legs crossed, in Camford's war room, using the full extent of his psi powers and the room's psi-sensitive construction to reach his much-missed kin. His cock throbbed at the thought of his shanna, but he could not relieve himself the morning after knowing her for the first time. Nothing but Georgia would ever sate him again. Fari knew this with a hopeless, angry certainty.

Judge me on my own merits, he psi-grumbled, feeling unworthy. So many mistakes in his past. And some at such a horrible cost. I have few merits beyond brute strength and speed.

That is far from true, Brother. Stay out of the past. You were but a boy then, and now — a man. A warrior who has given honor, blood, and bone for the Fleet, his people, and his world. Have patience with yourself, and patience with fair Georgia.

I have preached patience to you until I scarce have a throat, and you never listened. Fari's mental tone sounded surly even to him, but Ki's presence in his mind was soothing. Why should I give you credence now?

Because you are strong. You are wise enough to know I am right. Ki's soft laughter goaded Fari in a familiar, welcome way. And because you have no choice.

Fergilla.

Fergilla-poker. And as much as I would like to continue this stirring discourse, Brother, I have a ship full of Bandu rescues to return to Bandu-Mother before I can return to deal with the Outlanders.

Fari's eyes opened wide. "Bandu?" he asked aloud, still broadcasting his thoughts. "The OrTans are mad. What possessed them to take on such a cargo? Maybe one wild Bandu could be subdued on a skull slaver—but a group of them?"

The lizards need money to rebuild their fleet, and no doubt the Nostans offered a king's ransom for this tribe. Ki spoke with some difficulty, and through the psi-link, Fari heard screaming and the splintering of wood. Lots of Ardani cursing, too. Bandu royals, these. Queen Unk will owe us a favor.

If you survive the trip to claim it. Fari laughed. *Little Nostan fools. Why they insist on trying to tame the most vicious female species in the universe, I will never know.*

Ki went silent for a moment, no doubt wrestling with some of the fierce Bandu fighters. Bandu had little use for males, even Ardani warriors rescuing them from OrTan sex slavers.

How is Elise? Ki finally managed to ask. The tense desire for his shanna in his psi-voice came through clearly.

Fari felt a surge of compassion, followed by an odd jealousy. *She is well, Brother. Her belly grows and grows—your daughter will be a fine strapling, like Krysta at her birth.*

If Akad had not forbidden Elise to have sex until she delivers, we could—

Thank you for the thought. Fari knew Ki would have offered for Elise to relieve some of Fari's misery in the war room, with Ki in psychic attendance. And yet even the sweet Elise, as beautiful and sensual as she was, held no appeal to Fari beyond the normal brother-by-marriage interest. Fari had initially thought that attraction strong, but now, measured against the pull of his shanna, it paled.

I understand. Ki offered a gentle, non-teasing tone. Until I found Elise, I had no idea what it would be like either, Brother. My heart aches for you — but have faith. Georgia will recognize the truth soon enough. Her soul will give her no option.

May the universe hear you. Fari sent his brother a mental punch to the shoulder, then let the connection go as Ki once more went to battle with the Bandus before they tore Astoria apart.

In times past, Ki likely would have bedded several of the undomesticated females. Combat was a natural precursor for coupling in Bandu tradition, and many of Arda's warriors would be well-used and exhausted by the time Astoria dropped its hostile cargo on Bandu-Mother. Not Ki, though. Fari knew now, only too well, how his brother's heart, mind, and desire would be focused on Elise and Elise alone.

Such was the fate of a warrior who had found his shanna.

"Even if she hates me." He stood slowly, allowing the powerful octagonal design of the war room to bring his senses back in line.

His cock stood straight out against his breeches, painful in its single-minded demands.

Fari could masturbate twenty times in a row, and without Georgia's attention, his cock would simply swell back to unbearable dimensions.

He sighed. A walk in the woods. Some long overdue sparring. He needed to spend his energy.

And it is time for more potion. In reasonable measure this time.

* * * * *

"Well?" Elise's blue eyes sparkled as she splashed bubbles toward Georgia in Ki's huge bathchamber. "How was it? Details, woman. Details!"

"No." Georgia splashed back and felt herself flush. "I never kiss and tell."

They had chosen bath scents mixed by Akad to approximate Earth flowers and fruits—strawberry, raspberry, apple, and roses. Mixed with the steam, the enveloping warmth of the water, and the multicolored bubbles, the effect was dizzying and relaxing all at once. Georgia loved that the bathtub was big enough to swim in, and the swirling jets of water stroked her nipples and pussy in a most effective way.

Elise's heavy-lidded expression communicated her own enjoyment. "On Earth, you told me everything. Twice as much as I wanted to know. Why so shy now?"

"Oh, all right." Georgia rolled over and floated on her back. "It was…um, good."

"Good?" Elise's surprise filtered through the water in Georgia's ears. "It had to be more than just *good*."

Georgia grinned in spite of herself. "Okay. Yeah. It was awesome." Her pussy, still tender in a wonderful, satisfied way, ached under the bath's relentless jets. The sensation doubled as she thought about Fari, about the way he held her so tenderly, and fucked her so perfectly. "Are all Ardani men so well-endowed?"

"I think so." Elise leaned back in the water as Georgia floated back up and braced against the side of the giant basin. "Krysta says they are. I've seen a few naked ones around here, even the priest—but Ki and Fari have them all beaten, I think."

A flare of jealousy surprised Georgia as she thought about the fact Elise *had* fucked Fari—sort of. In that almost-way allowed to same-generation in-laws by Ardani custom. Oral sex, penetration other than vaginal—though Elise said some families shared sex more completely. It all depended on the agreement of the couple.

"You don't have a thing to worry about." Elise swam over and stroked Georgia's hair. "Fari only had an interest in me because of his link with Ki. Now that he's found you—"

"Stop." Georgia pushed away and kicked her legs under the water, suddenly unable to contain her energy. "Now that he's found me—what? He's forever smitten? Fari's soul won't rest until I'm married to him and fucking him every day? Blah, blah, blah. I've heard it all from Akad. Bullshit. Fari doesn't even know me, Elise."

Elise floated out to meet her. Before Georgia could slip away, Elise caught her shoulders and pulled her close. As Georgia's *pa* mingled with Elise's and rubbed across Elise's belly, Georgia felt an incredible bond of family, and a huge protective surge for the growing life inside her cousin.

Ilya, Elise and Georgia thought together, calling the unborn girl's name.

The baby stirred in response, kicking and punching against her prison of flesh.

"She won't wait much longer." Georgia reached down and rubbed the spot where Ilya fussed and wriggled.

"She's impatient. Like you." Elise kissed Georgia's brow, letting her lips linger long enough to increase Georgia's heart rate.

More than once since Georgia came to Arda and began to experience the total sexual freedom the planet offered—and especially since she learned of family-based sexual customs—she had thought of making love with Elise. Of being asked into Ki and Elise's marital bed.

"It will happen," Elise whispered. "In due time, after Ilya makes her debut."

The women shared a slow, gentle kiss as they floated naked in the humming water. Georgia thought about how Elise's lips were as soft as Krysta's, but more full and yielding. Fari's lips were firm, demanding—but not in a bad way. In a hot, possessive, mind-twisting way.

Georgia's pussy began a fierce ache even the water jets couldn't calm.

"Fari does know you," Elise murmured in Georgia's ear, keeping their body-to-body embrace. "Better than you think. He's seen some of your past, your hurts—even some of your art. He longs to understand you. And you told me how respectful he's being. Do you know how weird that is for him? Fari takes what he wants when he wants it. You, he's treating like some rare, fragile flower."

"Only because I won't fuck him if he doesn't." Georgia eased away from Elise, reluctant to let go of the comfort she offered. "All men are manipulators. You used to know that."

"I've learned differently now." Elise drew a soapy spate of bubbles over her chest. "Because I let myself be open to Ki and what he had to offer. I let myself know *him.* My God, Georgia. You've touched Fari's mind, his feelings—do you think he's hiding some dark side?"

"I—well—no." Georgia swam to the side of the basin and lifted herself out. "I think there are some dark corners in there, but nothing that would hurt me. It's just—the closer I get to him, the angrier I feel. And the crazier. Old stuff, I know—but I can't wave a wand and make it disappear."

Elise finished soaping herself. "So, what would it take?"

"If I knew that, I'd have fixed it a long time ago." The bath lost its appeal, as did everything in life when Georgia thought too hard about the past. About high school and her date rape at Chuck Sampson's hands.

Every time she came close to trusting a man, to wanting anything more permanent than a few fucks and a thank-you-ma'am—that old anger rose. She got suspicious. Too nervous to live in her own skin. And she kept waiting for the man to change into…into…an asinine, self-absorbed monster.

How to get past something like that—hell. Even her Earth therapists hadn't been much help.

Georgia got out and toweled off, oblivious to Elise's small talk and attempts to distract. She wondered absently where Krysta was, then remembered the talk of Outlanders and black feathers, burning barns and freaky religious messages. Krysta was somewhere doing her job as Arda's Captain of the Home Guard.

The bedchamber felt huge and empty as Georgia stepped back onto the cool marbled floor, naked except for her towel.

Maybe Krysta would swing by and pick her up for a little afternoon recreation. Georgia tried to get excited by the thought, as she would have only a week or two ago. She tried to think about experimenting with a few more Ardani warrior hunks, and even that held little appeal.

Georgia felt flat. Empty. Horny but wanting only one thing.

"Fari," Elise said, cutting into Georgia's reverie.

As Georgia glared at her distant cousin, Elise offered Georgia a large tunic and a pair of breeches. "These are his. I thought you might want to...um, keep them."

Still glaring, Georgia snatched the clothes.

Fari's strong, forest-like man-smell filled her senses, and in a fit of silliness, Georgia pulled his tunic over her head.

It came down to her knees, and Elise laughed.

"I wear Ki's all the time. With a belt. Can't wear the pants, though. I keep them under my pillow when he's away."

I would never... Georgia's thoughts trailed off as she held the soft, musky breeches.

Who was she kidding?

These were going straight to her room, and straight under her pillow.

The whys and why-nots, she'd work those out later.

Elise gave Georgia a see-you-later kiss, and Georgia headed for her own bedchamber. Camford's halls were deserted, since most of the warriors were out sparring and the women who weren't warriors themselves were off doing what women on Arda did — spar, ride, hike, climb mountains, learn — the possibilities were endless.

Fari's soft tunic felt delicious against her skin, and Georgia's desire for him increased tenfold with each step.

Take the stupid shirt off, one part of her mind demanded.

Never take it off, another part argued.

In the end, she left it on and belted it with a purple scarf. Feeling naughty and excited all at once, she didn't put on any shoes or underwear, and left her room without a backward glance.

Krysta, Fari, and Elise all be damned. It was a good day for a ride.

Chapter 8

Fari swung his barbed blade hard against his sparring companions. The four of them were deep in the forest, halfway between Camford and Browntown. Part patrol, part workout — this was just what Fari had needed to battle back the mating fervor, at least a little.

"You have slowed," one of the soldiers growled. "Methinks your mind stays more on a wet slit and big breasts."

Red rage blazed through Fari's better sense. He gripped a nearby branch and used it to swing himself at the insolent Markon. To hear Georgia reduced to such language — this fergilla would die a horrid, bloody death!

His sword connected with Markon's obsidian blade, and the crack and crackle made the two other warriors, Sai and Numo, howl with battle lust.

Slay. Destroy. Fari barely processed that he was trying to kill his under-keeper, the man who would take his place as Sailkeeper should he be lost in battle.

Markon sensed the change in Fari's mood and fought harder.

"I spoke in jest," the under-keeper asserted, climbing a nearby stump to give himself advantage.

"And with great disrespect." Fari's deranged growl made Sai and Numo snap to attention. They moved in immediately, intent on restraining their master.

Dizzy with the urge to destroy any and all who might insult his *shanna*, Fari took them all on, swinging wide pivots and making grand, piercing thrusts.

Thankfully none of his blows struck their marks before Sai managed to lung beneath a parry, grab Fari's ankle, and uproot him.

It took the three of them to sit on Fari's back until the wave of madness had passed.

"This is out of hand," Markon said with quiet deliberation.

Fari bucked beneath them, calming in half-measures and remembering Ki's similar senseless behavior on *Astoria*, after Elise's capture.

"Your mating fervor must be better managed, or you need to spar alone until it is settled." Markon's tone was infuriatingly logical, and his words were correct. Fari didn't wish to hear him, however, and gave one last mighty push from the ground.

Markon and the two other warriors held fast. "Give me your word, Fari. No more battle-soldiering until you have resolved things with your *Lorelei*."

Fari responded with a snarl. Yet even as he tried to reject Markon's wisdom, he knew it to be true. Lulled calm, distraction, obsession—these were ingredients for disaster and tragedy.

His mother's smile, radiant as she boarded the vacation schooner...

His father's affable handshake...

They trusted me, and I let them down. I let my own parents fly to an early death.

Perhaps Markon would be the better Sailkeeper, after all.

Fari kicked against Markon, then fell still. "No battles until the fervor abates. Agreed."

At that moment, a great shrieking and thunderous explosions smashed the silence of the wood.

Markon, Sai, and Numo were up before the first shocks died away, with Fari close behind them.

Blindly, they ran toward the chaos, swords drawn.

Thick, acrid smoke tore at Fari's eyes and throat. He coughed and blinked as branches smacked his shoulders and face. Vines made him stumble, but he managed to keep his footing as he plunged forward.

"That way!" Krysta's voice rose over the racket, and Fari heard the thundering sound of Chimera at full gallop.

As the four warriors burst into a clearing, Krysta and a patrol of Home Guard, mounted with weapons drawn, swept past them.

"The building yards!" Krysta cried. "The new ships!"

Fari and his group set out on foot behind the Chimera, running as hard as they could and damn near keeping up.

In a few stellar minutes, they broke free of the forest, to the western shore of Camford Lake, which fed into Camford River and quickly into the Arda Sea.

With each step, the smoke grew heavier.

Krysta waved her free hand and sword above her head, using psi-skill to part the dark, burning clouds.

Ahead of them, the building yards waited at the river's mouth. Roiling black fog obscured many of the building cradles and support structures—but the damage was obvious.

Someone had blown up most of the newer vessels.

A quick inspection told Fari that only his new ship remained. A small first-assault frigate he planned to name *Lorelei*, in honor of the women he loved.

Yard workers scrambled and ran. Some had burns, or burning clothing. The Home Guard was already fanning out into the melee, and Fari's three companions waded in as well. Overhead, a Home Guard speeder squadron sped in to assess the situation.

"Report!" Fari barked, aloud and in full psi-command.

Information trickled in rapid-fire.

Charges set deliberately.

Lorelei not rigged for explosion.

Thirty-six wounded.

Where are the priests? We need the healers!

A black falcon feather.

Several. One beside each destroyed ship.

Brother. Krysta's voice overrode the rest. *Come here, to the gates. You must see this.*

Fari turned to his left and strode to where his sister waited. The building yard's main gates, crumpled and smoking, hulked over a message etched in the dirt.

Vessels of war will not save you. Repent and believe, before it is too late. The Great Darkness is coming. I have left you one ship. Sail it into the sky in peace, and let us talk of saving our world.

"I will kill Weil with my bare hands." Krysta planted her sword in the torn ground. "Destructive, senseless fools!"

The Great Darkness. Fari shook his head. For years, the Outlanders had been prophesizing the end of time. Some doom would come from space and swallow the Ardani system whole, planet and person alike.

First, they pushed for migration to another home.

Then they demanded a return to the old knowledge. The old magic and the old ways. Surely the answer had to be in the ancient texts.

"Idiots. This will take stellar months to overcome." Fari clenched his hands at the sound of a late-arriving speeder. "We need guards on every town, every building yard, Camford—"

"Agreed." Krysta's wrathful expression spoke volumes. It had been years since the mainland of Arda faced such a direct threat, the recent Battle of Camford notwithstanding. "And I think we should—"

"Fari! Krysta!" Elise's panicked voice shocked Fari into wheeling around.

His sister-by-marriage was disembarking from the late-landing speeder. "What happened?"

Krysta reached her first and caught her in a protective embrace. "You should not be here. There are wounded, and the Outlanders may still be close."

Elise gripped Krysta's shoulders. "But, where's Georgia? She went for a ride in the forest a while ago, and when the explosions hit, I lost my sense of her—"

Fari heard no other words.

He grabbed Krysta's Chimera and mounted with the beast already on the move. They headed into the trees at a dead gallop.

Focused, breathing only to sustain life, Fari's mind opened wide, pushing through the hundreds of psi-conversations flying up from the building yards, the thousands of psi-inquiries coursing over the planet's surface. From bird to slinking creature in the grass, he searched psi-signature after psi-signature.

Geor-gia, his mind called, saying the name in a two-syllable rhythm. *Geor-gia.*

It was an old technique, a sort of psychic drumming, designed to reach through noise and confusion and establish a link with a willing mind. If only his shanna were seeking his thoughts as well.

Geor-gia. Geor-gia.

Nothing answered him.

Fari swore.

He should be able to sense his beloved in this state of urgency, even if she had her thoughts shielded.

Was she unconscious?

Had she been taken off-planet?

Everyone I love…I have no worth as a protector!

He urged his mount into a faster run. Trees loomed like opposing warriors, then flew by.

Help me!

Georgia's shout came all of a sudden, aloud and along psi-channels.

Fari nearly broke the Chimera's neck turning the beast back toward Camford.

Lead me, shanna! His answering call blasted from his mind as he thundered toward his beloved. *I am near!*

This time, the only response was a blood-chilling scream.

Chapter 9

Georgia Steel clawed and kicked and fought off two of the biggest men she had ever seen. They had black hair like Arda's warriors, but no *pa* marks. Instead, set center in their chests, were stones. Shining coal, or maybe obsidian.

And they smelled strange. Metallic—almost like gunpowder.

Her ears rang from the explosions. She tasted her own blood from biting her lip during their first assault, when they had yanked her off her Chimera.

The poor beast fled in terror.

Georgia held up her hands to scratch the first one who dared to take a step toward her.

"We do not wish to harm you," said the nearest giant. His words—wooden new-style Ardani, like he'd just learned to talk.

His companion bared his teeth.

"Yeah, well, if you take another step, *I'll* harm *you*." Georgia spoke Earth English and kept her hands up. Her heart hammered so hard she thought it would break her chest. Something nudged at her mind, a sound, almost like a clock ticking.

Fari, calling her name.

She tried to concentrate enough to answer.

"Come with us peacefully." The first man beckoned, still in stilted Ardani. He obviously had no idea what

Georgia had said. There was no mind-to-mind link at all, not even a rudimentary connection to allow them to understand each other. "You will not be harmed."

They started toward her, and Georgia screamed as loud as she could—in her mind and out loud.

Arms stronger than vise grips clamped around her shoulders, and then her legs. She tried to kick, hit, scream again—anything—but she was helpless as they lifted her like a log. Her breath choked to nothing. Images from the past rushed through her mind—images of fighting, for nothing, against someone so much stronger.

Even powered by rage and terror, she couldn't free herself. And yet her years of recovery and her months of finding strength on Arda rose like a wave inside her.

Not again. This will not happen to me a second time!

A meaty hand clamped over her mouth, and Georgia sank her teeth into it until she felt bone.

One of her attackers bellowed, and they dropped her.

She hit the ground, rolled, and scrambled to her feet just in time to see the blue flash of a wicked barbed sword.

"Fari!" A rush of relief nearly drove Georgia back to her knees.

The Sailkeeper of Arda did not answer her greeting.

He had waded in against the tree-men, sword slicing and gouging. The two giants might have been taller, but Fari was definitely faster.

The grim set of his mouth, the blaze in his eyes—this was more than doing his job. Georgia could tell this was personal. Fari was fighting *for her*.

And winning.

"Kick their asses!" Georgia hopped up and down, spitting out blood—hers and that of the giant she bit.

The big intruders never had a chance to draw their own swords. Howling and guarding wounds from Fari's blade, they fled into the trees.

For a moment, Georgia felt sure Fari would chase them.

He didn't. Instead, he stood between Georgia and the retreating men, gory blade drawn, until he was certain they would not reverse course.

Then he turned to her.

He was flecked with sweat and blood. His black tunic was ripped in several places, and dirt smears highlighted his face and hands. The fire of battle still sizzled in his eyes, but the rage quickly drained from his expression as he stared at her.

"Are you injured?" he asked in a quiet voice.

Georgia shook her head.

Fari sheathed his sword, then took a tentative step toward her, as if he feared she would run away from him, too.

A thousand reactions flicked like cue cards through Georgia's mind, ranging from thankful to sarcastic. Sarcasm would be typical. Anything to keep a little distance, preserve a little pride.

For what?

She shook her head again, startled by her own question. As corny as it sounded, having a man fight for her—really lay his life on the line and *fight* to protect her—that felt damned good.

Georgia discarded her well-rehearsed caustic remarks and did what she most wanted to do.

She hurried forward and threw herself into Fari's arms.

"Beloved." He caught her easily and held her, kissing the top of her head. "I was so worried."

"Thank you." Georgia realized she was shaking. "I— I—thank you!"

Fari cradled her, whispering comfort, offering his thoughts and emotions freely through their psi-link.

Georgia clung to him, body and mind, and before she knew it, sobs welled up. Painful sobs, from some cavern of despair deep inside her. Fari didn't flinch from her emotions. Quite the opposite, he stayed as steady as a rock.

I am here, shanna. Cry until the fear is spent. Nothing will hurt you now. And if I can prevent it, ever again.

It was so easy to hold on to this man. And even easier to believe him. Georgia let herself melt into his chest. She cried and cried, until exhaustion rendered her dry and limp in his embrace.

Still, Fari held her. The gentle press of his cheek on her head felt like medicine for her old wounds.

"Kiss me," she murmured, offering her mouth.

Fari brushed his lips against hers. "Come. Let me take you back to Camford. Elise and Krysta will be worried."

"I don't care." Georgia moved against Fari's muscular chest. "Kiss me."

Desire brightened Fari's midnight eyes, but he cupped Georgia's face in his hands. "Nothing would please me more than to lay you on this ground and make love to you until morning—but you were just attacked. You are frightened and vulnerable, and I fear you think you owe me something for your protection."

Georgia started to protest, but she was too stunned to speak.

Once more, Fari brushed her lips with his own. "Let me take you back to the castle."

Eyes closed, Georgia nodded.

Fari lifted her like she weighed no more than a child and held her close to his warm, hard body.

Georgia wrapped her arms around his powerful neck and held on, feeling the soft brush of leaves and blossoms on her skin as they walked.

Protected. Safe. Treasured. Respected.

She felt all of those things at once, and didn't know how to respond. Thankfully, Fari didn't require a response. He really wasn't doing this to exact any price from her.

Sha. Georgia toyed with the word in her shielded thoughts, wondering for the first time what it would be like to have this man beside her all the time. Day and night. She had never given marriage serious consideration before—and she wasn't sure she wanted to—but Fari tempted her to think about it.

* * * * *

Elise and Krysta met them at Camford's gates, along with two of the lesser priests. The healers immediately took Georgia from Fari, laid her on the grass, and began tending her cut lip and many bruises. She saw other Ardani citizens—workers and few warriors—also lying nearby. Many were burned, but all seemed to be recovering quickly.

"In the woods, it was Weil's personal guard," Fari explained to Krysta and Elise as one of the priests dabbed a paste on Georgia's lip. "I am sure of it. The bastard must have been planetside himself."

"Were they trying to—trying to—" Elise didn't seem able to form the words.

"No." Krysta sounded adamant. "They did not plan to rape Georgia. At least, I do not believe that to be true. The Outlanders are barbarians, but they have no history of misusing our women. What they do with their own is anyone's guess."

Fari agreed with a grunt. "They wanted an Ardani hostage. Something to give them bargaining power. Likely they didn't know Georgia held any importance to our family. If Weil wanted a Tul'Mar, he would have sent a small army."

"Ki and the Fleet are four stellar days from dock." Krysta glanced at the sky. "Once they arrive, the Outlanders will back off for a time. They know Ki will hear their concerns."

"Something feels wrong about this." Fari folded his arms and looked the part of a mistrusting cop. "It has a different…flavor. I do not think Weil is after negotiations."

Krysta smoothed her silver hair. "What then?"

"I think he wants a fight."

"I hope you're overreacting." Elise shivered.

"It would scarce be a match." Krysta snorted. "They have but a handful of vessels, and few in their ranks."

"That we know of," Fari muttered.

Georgia felt tension mount in her belly. Her head started to hurt, and to her great frustration, tears pooled in her eyes again.

Fari turned toward her. "Enough," he said to Krysta and Elise. "Georgia needs to go inside now."

Krysta nodded and walked over to Georgia. She helped her up with a soft tug, followed by a tender embrace. "I am glad you are safe."

"Me, too." Over Krysta's shoulder, Georgia saw Fari hug Elise and start to walk away.

An incredible chasm opened inside Georgia. She didn't want to lose sight of him. More than that, she wanted him to stay beside her. She *needed* him beside her.

Old voices tried to rise, telling her she needed nothing and no one.

She silenced them with a single mental plea.

Wait!

This time, her psi-request was not too late.

Fari stopped and turned around as Krysta let Georgia go. He didn't smile or act triumphant.

It might have been Georgia's imagination, or the intensity of her focus—but Camford's lawn seemed to go completely quiet. Elise and Krysta certainly did. They got out of the way, too, in one big hurry.

Fari's expression was one of relief as he covered the ground between them. Georgia didn't throw herself in his arms this time. She didn't have to. Fari picked her up with the same warm care he had shown her in the forest. His arms felt strong around her, and his hard chest made her think of his hard cock and the rest of his rippling muscles.

As he carried her up the steps into the castle, he whispered, "You can relax now. Some sleep will do you good."

Georgia pressed her face into his neck and ran her lips from the soft flesh under his ear to his rough, stubbled chin. Tasting him made her pussy ache. "Sleep wasn't what I had in mind."

Fari hugged her closer, but he didn't respond aloud or through their psi-connections.

Sometimes, the tall-dark-silent routine could be very frustrating.

* * * * *

To Georgia's great irritation, Fari ordered her a late lunch from a passing servant, took her back to her room, and tucked her into bed instead of ravishing her body. She had to admit she was tired, but not too tired for a little wild sex, if the gentleman was willing.

She patted the covers, squeezing her legs together to give her throbbing clit a little relief. "Why don't you get naked and get under here with me?"

Fari smiled. He sat beside her on the edge of the bed, studying her with those darker-than-dark eyes and stroking her cheek with one finger. "I was frightened for you today, beloved. It would crush my heart to lose you."

Can't lose what you don't have, the sarcastic part of her mind snapped behind what little shield she still kept between her mind and Fari's. Georgia blinked to clear her thoughts, and instead said, "I'm not planning to go anywhere."

A brief shadow covered Fari's face, but it passed as quickly as it came. Before Georgia could ask him what was wrong, he bent down and kissed her softly.

Her nipples beaded against her soft, borrowed tunic. It felt very erotic, to be dressed in Fari's clothes as he touched her.

He'd figure out soon enough that she had nothing on under that tunic.

Grinning, Georgia reached up and caught the back of his neck, holding him close. She ran her tongue along his bottom lip, enjoying his rich male flavor.

He groaned and rocked forward, and Georgia felt the proof of his arousal against her palm when she slipped her hand between his legs.

Please, shanna. I am in desperate need of a bath, and now...now just does not seem like the right moment.

"Why not?" Georgia squeezed his rigid cock through his breeches as he sat back up. "I eat my dinner, you take a bath...seems like the perfect moment to me."

"Even though I have had some—ah, incredible satisfaction, the mating fervor remains an issue, shanna. I would not wish to risk losing control with you so shortly after bitter reminders of your past pains."

"Let me worry about my past pains." Georgia stiffened and let go of his erection. "I'm finished with all that now."

Fari gave her an understanding smile, which pissed her off.

"Look. I asked you to come back here and be with me. Not baby me." Georgia gave him a little shove. "I can take care of myself, damn it. And I can make my own decisions."

"I—you—" Fari stood and ran his hand through his hair. When he looked down at Georgia, his expression reflected pain and confusion—and old, ghostly hurts

Georgia couldn't quite grasp. "Why do I make nothing but mistakes? All I want to do is care." His face flushed. "I want to love you, and be loved by you."

For once, Georgia was speechless. No snappy comeback so much as popped into her head. How could she lash back at a man who had the courage to lay his feelings so bare?

Besides, she had no idea what to say about her own feelings.

Tears rushed forward again, blurring Fari's stunning outline. Georgia swore under her breath, battling the wave of mingled sadness and joy threatening to overtake her.

"Why do you do that?" Fari's eyes narrowed.

Georgia sniffed. "Do what?"

"Fight your emotions." Fari shook his head. "If you have moved beyond what happened to you long ago, why do you deny such a large part of your being?"

"I never thought of it that way." Georgia wiped her eyes, unable to stem the tide of tears any longer. "After Chuck raped me, I had to be strong. Emotions aren't a part of that package."

Fari knelt beside the bed and kissed Georgia's damp cheeks. "It pains me to see you cry, and yet I do not wish to stop you if tears soothe your heart."

"Why are you so soft with me and so gruff with everyone else?" Georgia dabbed her eyes with the sheet. "I'd almost rather you be stern. Show me your tough side."

So I could stay mad at you, her shielded thoughts added.

Fari sighed and kissed her cheek again. "I cannot help but show you my true heart, shanna. Since I was young, since my parents were killed, I have shared your reticence to care. I have loved no one but Ki and Krysta, and recently, Ki's chosen mate—until you. For the Sailkeeper, at least this Sailkeeper, it is as you described. Emotions are not part of the package."

Wordless once more, Georgia nodded. The catch in Fari's voice as he spoke of his parents—something lingered there, but she didn't want to push him any more than he had pushed her. Pulling him closer, she buried her face in Fari's shoulder and sobbed while he gently ran his fingers through her hair.

What am I doing? she asked herself over and over, doing her best to keep her thoughts private.

Absolutely no answers came to her. Only the heat of Fari's embrace, and the occasional soft brush of his lips on her face.

Hours later, as Arda's two suns set on the splendid horizon, Georgia lay full and contented in Fari's arms. He had taken his bath. She had eaten her dinner, and a late snack, too. Fari had helped her change from the soiled tunic of his she wore to a clean one he brought from his bedchamber. They had talked for hours without fighting— no small task for the two of them.

Georgia had even showed the man her paintings.

No kidding, Elise. I really did it. She smiled to herself. Elise would be so ticked. Georgia never showed anyone her works in progress.

Georgia had done something else, too. She had agreed to go away with Fari for a few days, so they could have some private time and get to know each better. Away from prying eyes. Away from pressure.

They had not made love.

And Georgia had not asked Fari to leave.

She wanted to sleep beside him and wake up beside him in the morning, and see what that felt like.

Progress, she thought as the easy flow of his breathing lulled her to sleep. *Little steps get you there just as fast as big steps. Even if I'm not sure where "there" is supposed to be.*

Chapter 10

The next day dawned with hues of purple and gold. A "royal sky." According to Ardani legend, a royal sky meant good fortune for Arda's rulers.

Fari fervently hoped this would be the case.

He stood with Krysta and Elise outside his speeder's entry hatch, hand on the hilt of his infamous barbed sword. Georgia had already boarded, and Fari found himself glancing at the ship to make sure she didn't sneak out and flee.

One moment, his shanna seemed excited and relaxed. The next, she panicked and pushed him away. Her confusing behavior, coupled with Ardani mating fervor—Fari had seldom faced such complex challenges.

"Be patient with her." Elise folded her arms over her swollen belly. "Sex is a snap for Georgia. Relationships are hard."

"Much like someone else I know." Krysta gave Fari an affectionate punch in the shoulder.

He winced, but not from pain. From the truth in his sister's words. Mere stellar months ago, Fari would have scoffed at the thought of desiring only one woman. He would have laughed at the mention of marriage and beginning a family.

Now, as he touched Elise's stomach and felt his niece-to-be kick against his hand, Fari Tul'Mar dreamed of the day he would cradle his own firstborn.

His child.

Georgia's child.

A strong urge to hasten the process gripped him, and he imagined fucking Georgia in the front seat of the speeder.

The fervor. I have lost my mind.

"The Outlanders—" he began, trying to keep his thoughts focused.

"Fear not, Brother. We will not be caught off guard again." Krysta pushed a shock of silver hair behind her ear. "I have a unit in every village, and at every major construction site. Three units in constant patrol over Arda, just above the atmosphere. Ki is less than three stellar days from port, and until then, we can more than hold our own against Darkyn Weil and his rabble."

Fari gripped the hilt of his sword. "I still have a bad feeling about Weil's motives, and it bothers me that I do not know why he is challenging us."

"Maybe some of the Outlander Chimera herd took damage in the Battle of Camford." Elise glanced at the sky, obviously remembering the fierce starfight that almost cost her life, Krysta's, and Georgia's too. "When Ki gets back, he'll talk to Darkyn Weil and offer reparations."

Fari almost spat. "That pirate will accept no compensation if he has a mind for trouble. You must promise me, both of you—if the Outlanders attempt any further treachery before Ki returns, you will fetch immediately."

Elise leaned forward and kissed Fari on the cheek. "Promise."

"We can handle ourselves." Krysta pointed to the speeder. "Go. Save your sanity. Win your mate!"

Fari struggled with the feeling he was shirking his duties as protector of the family and fleet, but in truth, he was little good in either role while the fervor gripped him. No matter how he tried to concentrate, his thoughts strayed back to Georgia. Best to satiate the mating madness as soon as possible, then throw his efforts into contending with the Outlanders. Until then, Ki and Krysta would have to manage the situation.

Without further protest, Fari hugged his sister and sister-by-marriage and boarded the little ship.

The first thing he saw was Georgia, relaxing in the single passenger seat by the left console. Her flaming tresses covered the shoulders of her simple blue tunic — one of his — and the swell of her breasts made his mouth water.

She had on no breeches, and the tunic barely covered her thighs.

So much left to sample, to explore. By the stars, you are exquisite.

"You aren't so bad yourself," she murmured, eying him from head to toe. Her voice sounded slurred, and her heavy-lidded gaze made Fari wonder if she had taken some of Akad's calming potion.

"He made me." Georgia stretched, showing a feline grace. "Something about my *pa* mark, and my half-Ardani blood. Akad was afraid I might get a touch of mating fervor, and it might make me sick because I'm part Earthling, too."

Fari took a seat behind the speeder's controls, within arm's reach of his beloved. Thoughts of Georgia in mating fervor clawed his mind. The madness of mating males was legend, certainly—but an Ardani female in the grips of the fervor—now *that* was something to behold.

His cock throbbed as he fired up the engines and piloted the craft into Arda's clear, bright sky. As far as he was concerned, they could not reach Ammon Island fast enough. Ammon was Fari's private space, his very own slice of Arda's beauty, and he planned to share it with his future mate. Perhaps give her another glimpse of his truer, kinder heart.

And then, from the corner of his eye, he noticed Georgia absently fingering her nipples through the fabric of the tunic. The speeder shuddered as his hands slipped.

"Concentrate," he told himself aloud.

Georgia laughed. "What? Am I distracting you?"

Fari's voice deserted him. He glanced at her. She gave him a wicked grin, parted her legs, and rubbed herself.

Once more, the speeder bucked.

Fari ground his teeth and forced himself to keep his attention on flying the ship.

"Tell me about this Festival of Seasons everybody keeps talking about," Georgia said in a languid, husky voice. Her hand kept moving between her legs, and when her tunic shifted upward, Fari realized she had nothing on beneath it. His nostrils flared as her woman's scent filled the tiny cabin.

"The Festival is an old tradition," he managed in a tone as low and gruff as the speeder's engines. "A way for different family lines to mix and mingle, and for single citizens to claim mates by the old ways. It happens soon, too."

He cut his eyes to Georgia. She had pushed the tunic higher, above her hips, and her slit was clearly visible now. One of her fingers dipped into the swollen lips. Fari nearly bit his tongue in two. He wondered if his erection might rip his breeches.

"How does it work?" she asked. "Elise keeps insisting I'll enjoy it."

Fari felt a flash of fervor-related rage, but quickly reined it. "Eligible females are prepared by the old rites, and brought to Camford's grounds. Eligible males are paraded before them in groups. If a female favors one of the warriors, and he favors her, she tests him to see if he can bring her to satisfying orgasm."

"In front of everyone?" Georgia moaned softly. "How…exciting."

Fari didn't dare look at his shanna. He had already taken several wrong turns in the skies over Arda's thick forests, and they were currently sailing over the southern tip of the Nali Sea—at least three leagues off course for Ammon Island. "If they are soul's mates, they shout vows of claiming."

"That sounds delicious." Georgia's fingers moved faster, circling her clit, and Fari heard the slip-slip of wet flesh in heated movement.

"The Festival is foolish." He jammed at the autopilot, desperate to engage it before his brain exploded.

Georgia shifted in her seat, moving closer to him. "Why?"

"To submit to such scrutiny—no warrior with any pride would lower himself to such a cattle-call." Fari finally managed to turn on the ship's self-guidance system. He turned to Georgia just as she reached over, deftly unhooked his sword belt, and slipped her hand into his waistband.

"Now there's that arrogance again." She pulled out his cock and gave it a hard squeeze, and he groaned aloud. "Aren't you supposed to be flying this thing?"

"It...will...fly...itself...for...a...moment." Fari thrust against Georgia's hand as she stroked his rigid staff.

"What, no lectures about this being a proper or improper time?" She was half-turned toward him, and still working her clit with one finger. Her nipples puckered against the rumpled tunic.

Fari's *pa* caught fire as Georgia stroked him from sac to tip, toying with the bead of moisture on the end of his cock.

"You are trying to drive me mad," he said through clenched teeth. "I am not sure you are ready—"

"For what? A big bad Ardani warrior in full mating fervor? Without potion?" Georgia doubled the pressure on his pulsing staff. "You aren't my father. Why don't you quit playing daddy and let me decide what I can handle?"

Fari threw his head back and roared as she caressed his cock. He could feel his orgasm building, and Georgia's too. Their psi-link seemed doubled. Tripled. His shanna was relaxed from Akad's elixir. Her defenses were down, and her true passions came blazing through.

"Make us fly faster," Georgia whispered, slipping her fingers in and out of her slit, penetrating, fucking herself as Fari so wanted to fuck her.

Maddened by the fervor and his shanna's intoxicating boldness, Fari banged his fist on the speeder's panel.

The ship trembled as their speed increased.

Georgia lifted her tunic to expose her breasts, still massaging Fari's cock with great precision. She rolled one hard nipple between her fingers. "The faster you go, the faster I pump."

The thrum of engines blended with the rush of blood in Fari's ears. He kept punching the panel, and each time he did, Georgia moved her hand faster.

Outside, sky and clouds flew by in a blur.

"Faster," she demanded, once more rubbing her clit. "Yes. God!"

The speeder burst out of atmosphere into space as Fari came like a fierce volcano. Georgia cried out as she came, and Fari felt the sweet warmth of her satisfaction through their psi-connection. She was totally at ease, completely excited.

Raising her beautiful eyes to him, she turned loose his staff and cleaned his seed from her fingers.

He barely thought to slow the ship before they hurtled straight out of Ardani space.

Chapter 11

Georgia had never felt so turned on in her life. She had just given a warrior god a hand job at light speed. She couldn't wait to get to his island and really fuck him, hard and wild, over and over.

Akad was right, the back of her mind whispered. *I have mating fervor, too.*

Who the hell cares? the front of her mind argued. *A great fuck is a great fuck. No muss, no fuss. We have a deal. Just getting to know each other — zero strings.*

Fari guided the speeder back into the planet's atmosphere, re-entering with the barest of buffeting.

Georgia's pussy ached to have him inside her. She imagined his teeth on her nipples, his iron grip on her ass.

"Are we there yet?" she teased.

"Soon." Fari banked the speeder to the right, and Georgia saw the ruins of the sabotaged shipyard through the portal beside her.

"My new vessel, under construction," Fari told her in rasping tones. "The *Lorelei*. Next to *Astoria*, she will be the most powerful ship in the fleet."

Georgia nodded. The thought of Fari astride his ship's deck increased her excitement. Maybe she'd fuck him there, too.

I have lost my mind. She rubbed her forehead, fighting the strange craziness before it swallowed her better sense. *Before I know it, I'll be accidentally married, just like Elise.*

No, shanna. Fari's psi-answer came through firm and clear. *I will not trick you. There are only two other ways to marry, outside of Festival. The first is a claiming in battle, with later assent — as happened with Elise and Ki. The second is with a planned ceremony. I will not — cannot — marry you without your consent.*

"Okay." Georgia released a long breath. "There's just so much I still don't know."

"I will teach you." Fari's resonant voice made Georgia shiver with delight.

Fire flashed through her brain again, and she muttered, "I might teach you a thing or two, too, smartass."

Fari curled his lips in response. Georgia felt a surge of gut-level want, and she almost grabbed his cock again.

The speeder slowed, then began a gradual descent over crystalline waters, straight toward a small, heavily-treed island. To keep from wrecking them by attacking the pilot, Georgia studied it as they approached. Like Hawaii, only brighter. Bushes, rainbows of flowers, tiny lakes and streams — Ammon Island unfolded beneath her like photos from a dream vacation.

They touched down in a flat clearing, carpeted by emerald green grass.

Fari killed the engines and opened the hatch. "We are there yet. Pleased?"

Georgia felt the rush of fresh, warm air and smiled. As Fari turned and disembarked, she stripped off her tunic. Her *pa* felt like rivers of lava, and her pussy was on fire. She wanted to fuck — *needed* to fuck. Right then. Right there.

Her legs wobbled as she stepped out of the ship, and Fari helped her down with a grunt of approval. His grip slid from her sides to her ass as he spun her around and held her back against his chest. She faced the speeder and put her hands on the heated metal hull. In its opaque windows, she could see tropical trees and vines and heavy undergrowth all around them. The smell of salty ocean and the perfume of flowers filled the air, and Fari's intense eyes peered at her from his reflection.

He was still trying to humor her, to hold his animal instincts in check. Georgia could see it in the tense lines of his face. She sensed his raging desire in the thoughts he shielded from her, and a daring part of her wanted to free that tumult.

What would it be like to be at his mercy? To be fucked as hard and fast as she could stand?

"I want you." Georgia wiggled her ass against Fari's crotch as she pressed her hands harder against the ship's cooling hull. "Don't wait. I can't stand it."

Fari groaned and pressed his stiff cock into her cheeks. He shifted, moved away just enough to drop his pants and scabbard, then shoved against her pussy from behind.

Georgia bent over, still using the ship for balance, relishing the feel of his hard, naked flesh between her legs.

He reached down and gripped both of her nipples at once.

"Yessss…" Georgia shoved her breasts against his hands and spread her legs.

He teased her wet slit with the tip of his cock, rolling her nipples hard between his fingers. "You are so beautiful. I can scarce look at you without wanting to bury myself in your hot quim."

"You don't have to hold back anymore." She rocked back, gasping as the tip of his penis edged into her wet, ready pussy. "I don't want you to hold back."

Fari tensed. "Do not tease me, shanna. If I hurt you or frightened you, I could not bear it."

Georgia's head spun from the mating fervor. Blood thundered in her ears, and a primal part of her rose up to overpower her worldly concerns. Her mind seemed to split in two.

The sights and smells of the island, the feel of the speeder's warm hull, the sensation of outside air massaging her skin—everything melded with Fari's powerful body behind her. His cock pushed against her aching center, and Georgia shoved her ass back, impaling herself on his delectable length.

"Fuck me. God, yes." She bit her lip as he pinched her nipples, then thrust into her pussy hard enough to bend her elbows as she braced against the speeder. "Fuck me!"

Fari growled, and Georgia felt his powerful muscles flex. He filled her so perfectly. With each masterful stroke, he stretched her pussy to maximum and then beyond, to that point where pain and pleasure mingled.

A hot, malleable piece of wood. A burning metal rod. His cock felt better than anything she had known before.

"Fuck me!" Georgia slammed back against him, drawing him as deep as he could go. To her core. To the center of her being.

Fari let go of her nipples, grabbed her shoulders, and pounded into her, forcing her hard against him with each massive plunge.

"Yes. Yes. Yes!" Her cries kept rhythm with his driving thrusts. His *pa* sizzled against her ass and lower back. Her own *pa* crackled and flowed.

Fari's thoughts were incoherent, untamed. Georgia felt her own reason melting to nothing. Her pussy tightened, then relaxed, tightened then relaxed. Fari plunged harder still, sending Georgia's senses into a screaming whirlwind of pleasure.

And she was screaming. In her mind. Out loud.

Fari bellowed in return, filling her with his own molten heat as her orgasm nearly drove her to her knees.

He held her up, refusing to let her fall, refusing to stop fucking her until her body shook so hard she couldn't stand another second.

And then he pulled out, turned her around, took her down to the ground in his steel-strong arms, and settled between her legs. She had no time to protest. No time to think.

Soft island grass tickled Georgia's back as Fari dipped his cock deep inside her once again. Slow strokes. Deliberate. Building her pleasure again.

"You are so beautiful." Fari's rumbling words made Georgia groan. She felt hooked into his every movement, his every breath. He stared into her eyes as if reaching for her soul, and Georgia felt like he grabbed it.

His muscled thighs nudged her legs farther apart as he slipped in and out of her drenched pussy. Her nipples brushed against his smooth chest, and their *pa* touched and mingled.

Had anything ever felt this good?

Georgia raised her hips to meet Fari's thrusts.

"Wider," he whispered. "Open yourself. Let me fuck you like you've dreamed of being fucked."

Georgia moaned and spread her legs as wide as she could.

Fari caught her arms and held them over her head with one hand. With the other, he braced himself above her, just enough to spare her his weight. He moved against her, pushing deeper, and found her mouth with his eager lips.

In that second, Fari took complete control. Georgia knew she was at his mercy. She *wanted* to be at his mercy, and at that moment, she wanted to be *his.*

His tongue filled her mouth, and she loved his masculine taste, his earthy smell. Fari's grip tightened, and he fucked her harder. Faster. Like a well-oiled piston, ramming up and down, up and down.

Georgia screamed her pleasure into his mouth.

They glided on each other, coated in sweat. The musk of sex drove away all other smells.

Gazing into her lover's blazing black eyes, Georgia came with a bone-rattling jerk. Her body moved out of her control, bucking wildly. She couldn't think. She couldn't feel anything but her pussy clenching Fari's cock like a steel trap.

He emptied himself with a howl, once more flooding her with his hot, sexy essence.

Each time he moved, Georgia's entire being reverberated.

Gently, tenderly, Fari eased her down from dizzying heights, literally fucking her into a relaxed stupor. When at last he stopped moving, Georgia felt like she had no skeleton left at all. She had never known sex like this. She had never imagined an orgasm so total, so complete.

Tears of release slipped down her cheeks.

Fari kissed each salty trail, whispering how much he cared, how much he wanted to please her. How he would keep her safe, and cherish her for eternity.

My shanna. His psi-voice wrapped her like a soft sheet. *My beloved.*

For one heart-wrenching moment, Georgia wanted to say words she thought she would never say to any man. The three words formed in her mind, held back by tattered remnants of her old defenses.

Her mouth opened to speak that short, terrifying phrase. Her eyes fluttered, tried to lift—and then sleep's darkness claimed her.

Chapter 12

Two stellar days after landing in Fari's private paradise, Georgia lay in a rustic cabin, exquisitely sore from hour upon hour of hard, passionate fucking. She and Fari had barely taken time out to eat the exotic fruits and nuts the island offered, or even swim in the warm lagoon just outside the secluded retreat.

At the moment, she was nestled against Fari's chiseled chest. The rhythm of his breathing calmed Georgia's raging thoughts and kept her half-breed blood at medium simmer.

This "mating fervor" thing was no joke.

One second, Georgia felt like her old, level-headed Earth self. The next, her *pa* burned her like new brands and she became an Ardani bitch in heat, ready to eat through the bedsheets to reach Fari's perfect body.

Which person am I? Both? Neither?

Georgia stroked Fari's hair and sighed. She still hadn't faced the issues troubling her heart and mind.

Trust.

Did she trust this man? This giant of a sex machine?

Trust was harder than passion for Georgia. Almost harder than love.

Do I trust him?

The answer to that would have to be yes.

Not unequivocal, not at the depth she trusted Elise—but it was getting there. Fast. That realization alone disturbed her.

And then the bigger question.

Do I love him?

She imagined herself speaking those three small words. *I love you.*

Could it be true?

Did she really love Fari Tul'Mar?

Damn. She'd only known him for a few months—and half that time, she hadn't even liked him. Still, psi-connections offered a level of intimacy Georgia couldn't have imagined back on Earth.

She *knew* this man. This warrior. For the first time in her life, she had touched a lover with no lingering fears. No lurking shadows from her past, waiting to grab her from behind. Fari's open appreciation of her body, her intelligence and spirit, coupled with his freely-expressed desire and tenderness—those things dispensed with the typical man-woman games Georgia had come to despise.

Her chest ached from fear and pent-up emotions.

She cared about Fari. Of course she did. She had never met a more arrogant, self-assured, handsome, soft-hearted, persistent son of a bitch.

But she had just arrived on the most splendid alien world in the galaxy. Thousands of men would have her. All she had to do was crook a finger, and they'd come running. Why should she tie herself down to one guy so soon?

A year ago, Elise would have agreed with Georgia's hesitation. *In the end, all men are boring, Georgia.* If Elise had said that once, she'd said it ten thousand times.

But now, Elise was Arda's queen. She had a perfect husband and a baby on the way. She rode Chimeras, fucked constantly (when she wasn't in the last weeks of pregnancy and forbidden to do so by Akad), hiked mountains, flew sky speeders like an Indy 500 driver, and she was happy *all* the time. So happy Elise had abandoned their childhood pledges and rules.

Trust no one but each other. Take care of no one but each other…

Elise didn't even take time to ponder the mystery of how two half-breed Ardani kids, distant relations no less, turned up as orphans on Earth in the first place. Ardani females who just happened to be soul's mates to the Tul'Mar Clan.

Everybody had theories. Over-amorous traveling warriors, crashed ships, twists of fate — Georgia had heard it all. Even considered it herself. Only Akad seemed to share her deep curiosity about the "coincidence."

Sometimes, when they talked about it in their training sessions, the priest seemed distant. Almost worried. Georgia had intended to pursue the issue, but the Fari situation had overshadowed everything.

Here she was, socked away with her giant warrior lover, while who knew what was happening in the rest of the universe.

Georgia's body heated up as she glanced at Fari's naked form.

After they had touched down on Ammon Island and christened the landing pad, Fari had carried Georgia from the speeder to his cabin like some priceless treasure, in arms strong enough to lift horses. Her clothes had been left behind, and so had his. They hadn't gone back to get them, either.

She had only vague recall of Ammon's tropical forests, the gentle barriers of large-petaled flowers, and the suns-flooded cove cradling the cabin. Now, log walls surrounded them as they snuggled into a soft mattress set in a hand-hewn wooden frame. Fari had built the cabin himself, and all the furniture inside it.

Georgia had studied the carvings in the bedposts, and quickly realized Fari was an artist, too. All around the cabin's bedroom, the evidence lay in plain view. An expertly tooled rocking chair waited at the foot of the bed. Dozens of palm-sized totems and statues decorated windowsills and the mantel of the room's small fireplace.

He has a light touch with the wood. Georgia allowed herself an image of Fari hard at work on Ammon's rocky beach, carving some new fetish while she stood beside him, painting the seascape.

Stop it. She twitched as she admonished herself. *That seems way too...permanent.*

And then another whisper spoke up, that pesky little voice Georgia now blamed on her Ardani heritage. *So, what's wrong with permanent?*

Despite her best efforts not to give a real damn, Georgia's thoughts broke and reformed, focusing and refocusing on one thing:

Fari Tul'Mar.

He smelled of Arda itself, fertile and green and powerful. The steel of his muscle, the heat of his *pa*, the spark in his ebony eyes—everything about the man consumed her.

Georgia wanted to be angry with him for invading her private world so completely. She knew she should be afraid of losing control, of losing her heart. And yet she could think of nothing but making love to him again.

How would he fuck her? Where would he fuck her?

Her pussy ached for his cock.

I want him again. I want him all the time.

But he was snoring softly, too immersed in sleep to respond to her desire. After experiencing her own small measure of mating fervor, Georgia knew the poor man probably hadn't slept well in weeks.

As carefully as she could, Georgia eased out of the bed and tiptoed from the bedroom. The cabin was sparse and simple compared to the opulence of Camford, but Georgia liked it. Bedroom, den, bathroom, small kitchen—like an Earth retreat.

Afternoon light shimmered through beveled glass, casting prisms around the door as Georgia opened it.

As it had each time, the scene outside took her breath.

A crystal inlet, blue as the Caribbean, stretched between time-etched cliffs, out, out, out to the Arda Sea. On either side of the cove, small waterfalls tumbled over rocks, splashing and plunging into the waiting waters below.

Mesmerized, Georgia slipped out of the cabin, pulling the door closed behind her. Once more, she felt the tickle of Arda's soft grass on her bare feet, and the air's gentle caress on her naked skin.

I live here now. This is my world. My home.

The path to the cove was short but full of striking vegetation. Red blossoms spilled over purple bell flowers, and palm-like trees lorded over the tropical garden. Georgia paused half way to the beach, running her fingers over one of the palms' sandpaper bark. Vines hung from the tree's higher branches—and in fact, all of the palms had vines of differing lengths and color.

These were light blue.

Georgia grabbed one. "Me Tarzan," she grunted, then dissolved with laughter.

The vine felt soft against her skin, and she guessed it wouldn't hold her if she climbed and tried to swing like Jane did in the old television shows. Instead, she drew the silky fibers across her cheek and lips, then her nipples, then her belly.

Everything on Arda seemed created for enjoyment. For pure pleasure. Georgia closed her eyes and absorbed the whispering breeze, the gentle lap of waves in the lagoon, the heat of big sun and little sister, no doubt doubling the count of her freckles.

How many times can I masturbate before tall dark and well-hung wakes up from his nap? She straddled the vine. *It'll be an experiment.*

Shanna. Fari's psi-voice trickled into her mind, averting a startle. She turned around, and he was right behind her, grinning like an overgrown gorilla.

"Did you rest?" Georgia hunched on the vine, keeping her gaze locked with his.

Fari nodded. He licked his lips as she slid up and down the vine again.

Georgia felt her throat clench. Her *pa* pulsed, and Fari's carnal thoughts twined through her own.

Out in the landing clearing, by the speeder—the sex had been so wild. In the cabin, tender, passionate, and endless. Fari wasn't medicated any longer. He was all warrior now, raw and unchecked. His hard-on excited Georgia further, and she stroked herself faster with the vine.

"Want to watch me come?"

"No." Fari's voice had a rough edge as he reached out and caught her by the arm. "This time, it will be my way."

Georgia's heart fluttered. She thought about refusing him, but what was the point? She'd only fuck him later, twice as hard.

"Okay, hotshot." She dropped the vine and gave him her best wink. "Go for it."

Fari's grin looked more like a tiger's snarl.

He pulled Georgia close to him and spun her around until she faced the lagoon—but she couldn't see the water. Fari filled her gaze, her senses, even as everything melted to him, just him, as he kissed her deeply, parting her lips with his eager tongue.

She closed her eyes, welcoming his probe. The feel of his naked body pressed against her own made her ache for more, and still more.

Even your beard stubble—it feels so good on my cheeks. Damn. I can't get enough of you. The thoughts just slipped out, but Georgia didn't have time to regret them.

Fari took one of her wrists, even as his kiss deepened. *I will* never *have enough of you.*

Georgia felt the brush of fingers and silk—and then again, on the other wrist. Fari had bound her loosely with two of the hanging vines.

He broke from their kiss as she tested the ropes.

"Come back here," she demanded. "I'm not finished with you."

Fari quickly obliged.

Long kisses. Slow, and wet, and sensual.

All the while his hands traveled her hips, her pussy, her shoulders, and finally, her breasts. Fari stepped back and gazed at her, rubbing her nipples between his fingers.

"Do you trust me to please you?" His voice sounded like a tiger's purr.

Georgia groaned and pulled against the vines to support herself. Her knees wanted to buckle. Behind Fari, the Arda Sea pushed larger and larger waves into the lagoon.

"Yes," she whispered.

Fari smiled at her and studied her whole body as he tweaked her nipples over and over and over again. Georgia's pussy throbbed with each pinch.

"I know you fear attachment, beloved." Fari's deep voice doubled the pleasure Georgia felt from the relentless rubbing of her sensitive nubs. "But I do love you. I will ask nothing of you, but these feelings—I must express."

And before she could answer, Fari knelt before her and captured the end of one breast in his hot mouth. As he sucked, at first gentle, then harder and deeper as Georgia groaned and began to beg, she could see the waves crashing against the rocky beach below.

Throwing her head back, she moaned as he changed nipples and sucked just as hard.

"I can't take much more," she panted.

"But you must." He teased her clit once with his finger as he switched breasts. "I wish to take my time with you. You taste so good. So very good."

For long, long minutes, Fari did nothing more than suck her rock-hard nipples. His mouth felt like liquid fire on her skin, and his gentle nibbles made her cry out with shock and delight.

"I'm so wet." She thrust her breast farther into his mouth. "I think I'm going to come from just this."

Fari grunted his approval, captured her nipple in his teeth, and flicked the end hard and fast with his skilled tongue.

"Yes. God." Georgia arched forward, once more pressing her tender flesh against his lips.

Fari gathered the other breast and pressed it into the first. Then, holding the nipples together, he sucked them both at once.

Georgia jerked against the vines, moaning as a small orgasm rattled her.

Skillful as always, Fari rode out Georgia's shouts and kept up the pressure on her nipples until he fueled Georgia's desire all over again. Then he moved his kisses to her belly, and lower, to her come-soaked mons.

"I want to taste you," he murmured. "I want to fuck you with my tongue until you beg me to stop."

Passion washed Georgia in short, face-flushing shocks. She doubled her grip on the vines and spread her legs as wide as they would go.

In one fluid motion, Fari lifted her from the ground. He put her legs on his shoulders, leaving her suspended from the vines even as he braced her weight with his powerful arms.

Georgia felt like she had landed in the world's most erotic swing.

Fari parted the lips of her pussy with his tongue, moving them back with gentle strokes until her clit was completely exposed.

Any second, he would touch it.

But he didn't.

He just held her there, legs about his shoulders, rocking gently, clinging to the vines and pleading for relief with each whimper and sway.

She ground her teeth. "Stop teasing!"

At last, he licked her throbbing center.

Georgia screamed like she was dying. Her body acted outside her conscious control, arching her hips into his face.

Fari's strong hands continued to brace her at the hips as he pulled her forward, sucking her clit into his mouth just as he had sucked her nipples. He caught it tenderly between his lips, then used his tongue to hammer dead-center on the delicate nub.

So much pleasure it was almost pain.

Georgia's breath came in ragged gasps. She swung in closer, then pulled back a bit. Each time, Fari drew her inside his mouth, nursing her clit like a juicy strawberry. His tongue felt like a hot, wet finger on high speed, hitting the spot with relentless accuracy.

Georgia lost it. "Damn. Damn that's good! Ah, God. Don't stop. Damn!"

She wriggled and bucked and came faster than she wanted to.

No matter.

Fari kept suckling her, laving the tender flesh, drinking her juices with heated groans of delight.

Orgasm after orgasm rocked Georgia, until she indeed pleaded with him to stop the torture.

"Time to fuck me. Now." She swung herself back. "Before I lose my mind."

Fari slid her hips down in a flash, until her legs wrapped around his waist. Holding her gaze with his blacker-than-black eyes, he moved her to position his cock, then yanked her forward, burying himself womb-deep in her pussy.

Georgia let out a low moan of pleasure as her quim expanded to take his iron-hard length. He *belonged* inside her, like the perfect part in a perfect sexual engine.

She clenched him as hard as she could.

He stepped back, just enough to leave her hanging on the vines, thighs locked around his hips. And then he grabbed her ass and slammed her against his groin.

"So wet," he murmured. "So soft. You fit me, shanna."

Beyond coherent noises, Georgia closed her eyes and surrendered herself to the incredible sensations.

Fari fucked her hard and fast. The vines whispered and rustled above her, and she heard herself swearing, cursing, demanding that he make her come, demanding that he make it last forever.

Shanna. *My beloved!* He fucked her harder still. Deeper.

Georgia ripped her hands from the vines and threw herself forward, grabbing his shoulders for dear life. Each silken plunge seemed to reach the center of her being.

Their *pa* marks joined in a river of sparks, jolting them both.

"Now. Now!" Georgia pounded his shoulders, and Fari let her weight fall hard against his groin.

His hot seed exploded into her pussy as the walls contracted. Georgia came at the same second, clenching her legs and milking him dry. Thrusting and thrusting until she simply couldn't move.

Fari seemed frozen in place as well. He held her there without effort, in the middle of the jungle-beach. His cock felt like heaven inside her, and she never wanted him to pull out. Once more, a breeze ruffled leaves and petals, tickling Georgia's bare shoulders and back. From the lagoon, the gentle rush of water sounded like a lullaby.

"I love you, shanna." Fari's voice was just as peaceful and right as the rest of the natural sounds.

Georgia held him tighter and squeezed her eyes shut.

"*Sha.* I—I love you, too."

Chapter 13

Fari Tul'Mar felt like he had entered a time of dreams.

Morning sunlight bathed the Ammon lagoon, and Georgia stretched beside him in the soft beach grass. He faced her and stroked her freckled skin from neck to hip, watching the slow rise and fall of her breath.

Through their psi-link, Fari knew her dreams were of him, and of painting. Painting him, in fact.

Fari smiled and kissed Georgia's shoulder. She had tanned to a fine brown, tinged with the flush of health and happiness. A stellar day had passed since his shanna first spoke words of love to him. She had yet to repeat them, but her prickly demeanor had softened to that of a pleased cat.

At the moment, she was well-sated from a breakfast of fruit, nuts, and sweetbread, followed by a slow *kon'pa*, the Ardani dance of life—and an equally slow coupling on the higher beach, near the cabin. Neither of them had worn clothing since they landed, as it should be in a couple's new-mating time.

"But this is not our new-mating time," Fari reminded himself quietly. A mix of pain and anguish twisted in his belly. All along, Georgia had been clear about her wishes, intents, and desires. Commitment and marriage were not among them.

Besides, after Fari's many past failures protecting those he loved, perhaps he was less than worthy of such sentiments.

And yet, Georgia had told him she loved him.

How can I win you, my beloved? Fari flicked a lock of flaming hair from his shanna's face. If this were Elise and he were Ki, Fari would simply toss his woman over his shoulder and make off with her.

But Georgia and Elise, despite their friendship and kinship, were two very different women.

If Fari wed Georgia without her knowledge or consent, or attempted to keep her captive, or even threw her over his shoulder without her first requesting it, he doubted he would have a cock to fuck her with the following morning.

This wild thing, this *Lorelei*, she would get him in his sleep. With both of the legendary ruby blades hanging in her bedchamber back at Camford.

He loved that about her—the spirit and fire. Fari loved everything about Georgia, from her wit and intelligence to the way she curled her toes when he kissed her. Her past trauma had not defeated her. She fed on it, as if to spite her attacker—this "high school" man named "Chuck."

A fergilla I will have a long conversation with one day. Fari thought of his barbed sword and smiled again, this time in a carnivorous, dangerous way.

Georgia stirred and grumbled, then punched him softly in the chest. "Your thoughts are noisy."

"My apologies, beloved." Fari carefully shielded his plans for Chuck of Earth, who one day would live to regret harming women. "Do you plan to sleep our day away?"

"Give me a reason not to." Georgia's eyes remained closed, but her hands grew active, tracing first Fari's stubbled cheeks, and then his heated *pa* mark across his chest, then down, toward his cock. "Ah. There's a good reason. A nice, thick, hard one."

"Always." Fari leaned forward and kissed his shanna, even as her fingers closed on his rigid length. She could please him so intensely, so quickly, and her appetite was near insatiable.

Georgia massaged the sac at the base of his cock. "I like how this feels in my hand."

Fari bit her lip gently, then let it go. "I enjoy it as well," he managed, though words were becoming difficult.

She moved from his bollocks to the base of his cock, circling, gripping it and sliding her hand up to the sensitive tip.

"Like silk, but hard as stone," she murmured. "God, I've never known a man like you."

Heat consumed Fari as his world became the movement of Georgia's skillful hand.

"How many women have you fucked? Fifty? One hundred? Probably three times that many."

Georgia's quiet inquiry took Fari by surprise. He had no shame over his prior relations, but he feared angering his shanna. Earlier experiences with Elise had taught him much about the jealousies of Earth females—and this private time with Georgia had been so perfect. Fari hated to spoil it, especially with her fist clenched on his manhood.

I scarce can think, beloved. You are not playing fair.

"Mmm." Georgia speeded her strokes, bringing him closer to orgasm. "Then it's probably more like four hundred. Or maybe you don't even know."

None compare to you.

With four rapid tugs, she dragged him to the edge of bliss — and stopped. Fari clamped his teeth together. Sweat broke over his brow as she gripped him harder, and harder still.

"How do I know that?" Georgia asked. She sounded sultry. Teasing. Completely maddening.

"Because I do not lie." Fari covered her hand with his. Georgia drew a sharp breath, but her thoughts communicated excitement and the thrill of challenge.

"Because you may read my thoughts whenever you choose." Slowly, Fari moved her fist up and down his stiff cock. She offered some resistance, a token, but that only increased the sweet pleasure.

"And because however many women came before you," Fari said as he pumped himself harder with Georgia's fingers, his words escaping in ragged gasps, "there will never be another without you."

Georgia's eyes widened.

Fari came with a powerful spurt, and his shanna bent forward and drank his seed. Her thoughts were a jumble of happiness and fear — but they were not closed to him.

Georgia's heart thumped against her ribs as she rose from sucking Fari dry. His cock was already getting hard again, which thrilled her to no end. She felt like a nervous teenager, having sex for the very first time. There they were, stretched side by side, naked body to naked body, on an exotic island, on the most exotic planet she could imagine, and she could fuck him any time she wanted, any way she wanted, as often as she wanted.

There will never be another...

Fari had committed to her, and he hadn't asked for anything in return.

He leaned down and suckled her breast, rubbing his tongue across the hard, pebbled flesh. Shivers of pleasure gripped Georgia, and she ran her fingers through his long, thick hair. Her other breast literally ached for his mouth until he gave it attention. Georgia let him toy with the sensitive nub until she couldn't stand another second, then pulled his head up to kiss him.

His mouth covered hers possessively, yet with infinite tenderness. Georgia parted her lips and joined her tongue with his, enjoying his male taste, his male smell, and the feel of his arousal against her belly.

Fari kissed her until she wanted to cry from his sweetness, then smiled as she pushed him back far enough to say, "I want you inside me. Now. Please."

His rumble of approval made her shiver again.

Georgia moved forward and lifted her leg over his hip, and his dark eyes captured her completely. With no teasing, he slid his cock inside her wet pussy, grabbed her ass, and pulled her as close to him as she could get.

The sensation of his thick erection buried in her hot core made Georgia groan. She closed her eyes, but he whispered, "Keep them open. Look at me while I make you come."

Fari's low, sexy voice made Georgia twice as wet. She forced her eyes open and lost herself in his intense gaze.

They arched together slowly. Each thrust seemed to take him deeper into her quim, farther into her soul.

Georgia's nipples rubbed against his hard chest as he ground himself against her, moving her with his powerful hands.

In that moment, Georgia joined with him, completely and perfectly. She felt deliciously *his*, as if no other woman could tame his wild warrior's spirit. If Fari had pronounced them married, she might not have cared.

Deeper. Somehow he went deeper into her pussy, and just fast enough to increase her arousal. His eyes bored just as deep into her consciousness. "So tight, shanna. Such a good fit, from head to toe. You were built for me."

Georgia tried to speak, but her voice failed her.

"Tell me what you feel." Fari rocked her back and forth with his hands on her hip and ass, raising her up and down on his throbbing cock. "Scream it when you come."

The thrum of his voice pushed Georgia closer to climax. Her heart kept rhythm with his skillful strokes. And still he stared at her. Into her.

Georgia's face flushed.

She knew she could fuck a thousand men, and never find a better lover. Or a better love.

Hearing her unshielded thoughts, Fari fucked her harder. "You are mine. I will wait as long as it takes for you to know that. For you to believe in me, in us."

"Oh—my—God." Georgia's words came in choked gasps. Every nerve and muscle in her body burned with her building orgasm.

Fari's eyes. Those eyes! His firm male body. His hot, hot cock, pleasing her like no man had pleased her before.

Her toes curled as Fari pumped into her pussy. One more stroke. Maybe two.

Heat rushed from her center, consuming her flesh and her senses. And still he stared into her very being. His muscles tensed, and Georgia's involuntary spasms shook her with incredible force.

"I'm coming." Somehow she kept her eyes open as an earthquake of pleasure rocked her without mercy. "Come with me."

"Say it," Fari demanded, keeping a tight hold, fucking her fast, then slow, fast then slow, making her orgasm last and last.

Georgia gripped his shoulders. "I love you. I love you!"

Fari groaned, filling her with his hot essence as yet another orgasm shook Georgia.

"I love you, my shanna." His murmurs sent new rounds of shivers along her spine as he eased her through the aftershocks, then settled her against his shoulder.

Georgia squeezed her legs together, holding his spent cock in her pussy. She felt insanely territorial, and she knew she never wanted to let him go.

Fari rolled her to her back, holding his weight above her.

Incredibly, he was getting hard again. Georgia thought she might die from the sweet exhaustion.

Was it possible to be fucked into oblivion?

She wasn't sure, but she was ready to find out.

Fari moved against her once, and she moaned.

"Will you...will you consider marriage?" he asked in the softest possible way.

Georgia arched her hips, drawing him farther inside her.

She didn't know what to say. Or she didn't know how to say it through the wall of fear suddenly wrapping her mind.

Obviously sensing her hesitance, Fari concentrated on fucking her instead. This time, his eyes were closed. He leaned closer to her, and as their *pa* mingled, Georgia had the dizzy feeling of her sensations and his, too, and she loved it.

She loved him.

"You fuck me so, so good." Moving wildly, out of her own control, Georgia bucked against him with each thrust.

Fari growled and rammed into her quim. Georgia sensed his building frenzy, and she wanted it.

"Yes. Fuck me as hard as you want. Faster." She grabbed his sides, digging her hands into his sizzling *pa*.

He roared and slammed into her with feral abandon.

So deep. So perfect. Pain and pleasure blended with a sense of total possession. Georgia arched against him, higher and higher, losing track of time and space. The soft, grassy ground seemed to spin beneath her.

"Mine," he bellowed with each hammering thrust. "Now. Always!"

"Take me, then." Georgia spread her legs as wide as she could. "Take me!"

Fari pounded her pussy then, shouting with each movement.

Georgia shouted with him. She felt herself sliding backward in the grass, helpless against his force. She wasn't scared. She wasn't triggered. Just excited beyond imagination.

"Fuck me! Fuck me, damn you!" Her head whipped back and forth as she came in a hot, throbbing explosion.

Fari's orgasm followed hers only moments later, and once more she felt his heated eruption filling her to the brim.

Before she could stop him, he pulled out in a rush and fell on his face beside her, panting.

Georgia groaned with the effort of movement, but she managed to roll to her side and trace the outline of his trunk-like back muscles.

"About what you asked, about marriage…"

Fari took a deep breath and held it. He felt so incredibly still, like a warrior statue, waiting for her words to free him, and —

And the roar of a speeder's engine shattered the island's peaceful silence.

Georgia startled so badly she almost rolled to her back. Fari leaped up so fast he shocked her a second time. Face grim, he scooped Georgia into his arms like a kitten and carried her into the nearby trees and brush.

"Who —" she began as he set her on her feet, but his mental command cut her short.

Wait. Friend or foe — I cannot tell.

Chapter 14

Fari held Georgia behind him, shielded by the trees. Her nearness, the light scent of her womanhood — these things made his battle blood flow all the hotter. If only he had his sword.

Damn. It was at the shuttle landing pad, with his clothes. *Well, no matter.* Fari flexed his muscles. If anything or anyone with ill intent came near Georgia, he would tear them apart without benefit of weapon. He would not, *could* not lose another family member to his short sightedness.

The island-invading ship was definitely an Ardani speeder. It jolted down on the edge of the lagoon, back rudders first, then front.

Krysta.

Fari relaxed a fraction. Only his sister rode a speeder like a Chimera, rearing and bucking at will.

In seconds, the speeder's side hatch opened, and Krysta vaulted into the water with an ungraceful splash. Her mental curse made Georgia giggle and grab Fari's waist. "Stand down, soldier. I think this one's harmless."

"Hmph. You did not grow up with her." Fari led Georgia from the trees and hailed Krysta with a wave and a psi-greeting. The sun felt hot on his naked skin, but not as hot as Georgia's soft breath on his shoulder.

There you are. Krysta's thoughts were clipped as she wheeled around and headed up the beach. *You have been psi-blind for hours. Stellar days!*

I have been occupied. Fari shook his head. Patience had never been Krysta's strength.

We have been occupied, Georgia added, snuggling closer to Fari. *That was the goal, wasn't it?*

Krysta approached like a charging fergilla. Her tense voice rose above the quiet lap of lagoon waves, shattering all illusion of humor or teasing. "The Fleet was delayed on Bandu-Mother. Ki is still a half-stellar day from port, and our skies have filled with Outlander vessels. Thirty. Maybe more. Most appear to be salvaged cargo ships, but a few are restored frigates and speeders."

The remnants of Fari's mating fervor cleared in a rush as he straightened himself and let go of his shanna. "Have they fired? What of the Guard? And the positions—"

"They are not in typical attack formations, and not in strategic locations." Krysta stopped directly in front of Fari. Her drawn face communicated more than a thousand recriminations. "Most are orbiting above Camford. I have positioned a net of Home Guard ships around them."

"If they have even one trained gunner on the salvaged frigates..." Fari trailed off as his mind jammed with possibilities.

"Where's Elise?" Georgia stepped between them. "Is she safe? What about the baby?"

Krysta's intense stare softened. "Elise is at Camford. I have located her in the Guard Captain's quarters next to the war room. It is the most secure location. Akad feared the psi-flow of the war room itself would be too much for her."

Fari rubbed his fist in his hand. "Her time draws near. Is the priest with her?"

"No." Krysta shook her head. "He is with the rear Guard, between the rogue ships and open space — awaiting Ki's arrival. I wanted him off the ground in case of full assault. We will need our healers in the air."

"This is bad, isn't it?" Georgia scuffed her foot in the grass.

"Possibly." Fari turned and took his beloved in his arms. He wanted to kiss her deeply, but that would only arouse him and distract him from grim purpose. He settled for a loving brush of her cheek, which she accepted without protest. "Go to the landing pad. Gather your things quickly, and Krysta will deliver you to Camford."

To Krysta, he said, "I will close up the cabin and go to the building yard. Have the forward Guard attempt contact with the Outlander ships — see if we can discern their demands. Meanwhile, you land in the forest, at the Tuscan Platform."

Krysta winced at the reference, at the thought of visiting the place where their brother was so nearly beheaded mere stellar months ago, but her thoughts indicated she understood his reasoning. The Platform was one of the few places around Camford where they could conceal and protect a speeder and still have easy takeoff.

And at the building yards waited *Lorelei*, Fari's first-assault frigate under construction and yet flight-worthy. It would be near suicidal for one man to attempt to pilot her, but Fari was a Tul'Mar. His gift was strong, and Ki would lend what psi-energy he could across the leagues still separating them.

If the Outlanders attacked, if the Home Guard was outmanned and outgunned, a surprise flank maneuver might be their only hope. A slim hope, but better than none at all.

Minutes later, still naked but with his clothes and sword at his feet, Fari piloted his speeder away from his perfect island and his perfect time with Georgia. So much progress—and yet she still had made no commitment to him.

And yet, before Krysta came, she asked about marriage.

Fari's cock stiffened.

He swore and forced his thoughts to the present, to the problems at hand. Nervousness in battle was not a factor. Fari tended to be at his best when under pressure, in hopeless situations. Speed and wit over brawn. He had his advantages.

And yet he had never had so much to protect. Such important people to defend.

Georgia was with Krysta now. If anything happened to them...

No. I will not consider that possibility.

Flying faster than any Home Guard ship should fly at surface level, Fari made a quick pass over Camford, then swooped even lower, in case the Outlander ships had any sort of rudimentary detection devices.

Thank the universe they were not psychic, or all of this would be pointless.

Almost clipping treetops, Fari hurtled back toward the building yard. He could sense the strange brew of misfit ships above him, and his extra senses told him they were armed and well-manned. Well-womaned, too. Many life signatures. Many engines. Many sails. Some strange energies he could not even identify.

And yet, no urgency. And odder still, no overt malice.

What are they doing? What could they want?

Fari rubbed his hand over his eyes. If not for the mating fervor, he might have been more on top of the Darkyn Weil problem. Or he could have assisted Ki with the drop-off of Rescues to Bandu-Mother. That certainly must have been a complex proposition.

What good was he to the Fleet, to Ki—to Arda— besotted as he had been?

But it is natural, he tried to convince himself, as he once had to convince his brother, who suffered a similar fit of guilt after long days of obsession with Elise.

Nothing can be done for the past now. Only the present, and the future. Fari's eyes narrowed as the building yards came into view. He punched the companel to slow the speeder and eased over the ruined docks.

The saboteurs had done a fine job mucking up the main Fleet construction site, but Fari's sleek and efficient *Lorelei* had already received her *pa* coating. A simple explosion could not harm her. She looked fit and ready, albeit slightly under-rigged. The construction was nearly finished.

Finished enough, he hoped.

Fari landed the speeder as close to tree cover as he could. He jerked on his pants and tunic and strapped on his sword. After one long, slow breath, he slowly called up one long, remembered image of his shanna, naked, waiting to hold him upon his return, then he disembarked.

Keeping all senses trained on his surroundings, he rushed across the open space between trees and remnant docks, leaped over gaping holes in planking, gripped *Lorelei's* tie ropes, and climbed aboard *Lorelei's* slender decks.

As fast as he could, he released her moorings, ran to the con room, and engaged her ion engines. The immediate, smooth hum of inertial dampers and rising containment fields greatly relieved him.

Lorelei was not only intact. She was functional. Her *pa* coating resonated with Fari's *pa* mark like an arrow joining with target. The ship shuddered at his presence, then drifted free of her docking, awaiting command.

Without hesitation, Fari headed for the center of the deck and climbed the rope ladder to the observation nest at the top of the center mast.

All three sails puffed at his will, but the ship remained still. She would fly when he told her to fly.

In position, Fari informed Krysta through a direct, focused psi-link. *And you?*

Landing the speeder. Krysta's dark, shielded tone made Fari grip the smooth, cool sides of the nest.

What is wrong?

Krysta remained silent.

Fari pressed his thoughts toward hers. *Tell me, Sister! This is no time for games.*

I—uh, when you sent Georgia to the landing pad to gather her belongings, she apparently did not do so. At least, she did not return to me.

For a moment, Fari could make no sense of Krysta's statements, and then truth struck him like a ragged wind. *She…did not leave the island with you?*

A surge of misery preceded Krysta's response. *No.*

Then Georgia is still on the island? Unprotected?

Another wave of ill feeling flowed across their psi-link. *I do not think so, Brother.*

Fari pounded the sides of the nest hard enough to smash a structure of lesser design. "Then where is she?"

And even as he broadcast the question, he knew the answer.

Chapter 15

Georgia hesitated on the rope ladder leading up to the "observation nest," as Fari had called it. On Earth, it would have been a "crow's nest," or something like that. Whatever the name, Fari was up there, above her head where she couldn't see him, and she could sense that he was more than a little ticked.

A light breeze enveloped Georgia's naked body. Rough ropes scrubbed against her nipples, palms, knees, and feet.

If he ties me to this, I'm in big shit.

Soooo, she hadn't told him a few of the secrets she'd been learning from Akad. Like how her extra *pa* gave her stronger mind-shielding when she willed it, among other things. She wasn't much good at enhanced psi powers yet. Hell, she could barely manage basic psi powers. Still, she had managed to stow away on Fari's speeder, blocked herself from his awareness, and followed him onboard a war frigate without him detecting her presence.

And now, she was hanging naked on a bunch of ropes, a hard wooden deck below her and a furious warrior above her.

Brilliant idea, Steel. One of your better plans.

"What in the name of five black holes are you doing on this ship?" Fari's resonant bellow made the rope ladder shake.

Georgia gripped it with both hands and climbed, even though half her brain suggested pulling a Tarzan over to the next sail, shimmying down, jumping overboard and running for her life.

She finished the scramble to the observation nest with a few well-placed steps and tugs. When she reached over the side, Fari grabbed her by the wrists, hauled her inside, and yanked her hard against him.

Georgia felt suddenly small against his muscled bulk, and her heart drummed against her ribs. Fari shifted his weight, and his sword hilt poked her hip. She winced.

The man was so mad his whole body shook. Georgia had never seen his face so red, even after hours of non-stop lovemaking on the island. Old defenses battled with new feelings, and for a moment, she wanted to slap him. Tell him off. Suggest he go fuck himself.

Instead, she started to cry.

Fari frowned and eased his grip. "Why did you come here?" he repeated in a dead-quiet voice.

Georgia turned her face away, hating the burn in her cheeks. Instinctively, she blocked her thoughts from him again. "I don't want you to leave, to go into battle. But I know you have to. I just wanted to say—I just wanted…"

"It is not safe here." Fari cut her off with a sharp, commanding tone. A lancing pain between the eyes told Georgia he was trying to force through her psi-barrier. "Go to Camford immediately."

This time, old anger won out. "Screw you, you arrogant prick." Georgia pushed hard at Fari, mind and body. He stumbled back as if she'd hit him.

With a jerk, she freed herself and fell against the far side of the observation nest. "I've told you once already, the day we left for the island—quit playing daddy. You aren't my father. I go where I choose, when I choose, damn it. And damn *you*. I choose to be here."

Fari shook his head and rubbed his temples, clearly feeling the effects of her unleashed psi-strength. When he looked at her again, it was with considerably less command and entitlement.

Better. Progress. Georgia sighed and righted herself. "Look. I love you, okay? You're a soldier, and you're going off to war. There's stuff I didn't say. Stuff I *need* to say. And you didn't give me a chance before, back on the island."

"I...apologize," Fari muttered, unbuckling his sword belt and laying it aside. Georgia could tell he was choosing his words with caution. His thoughts were open to her, though not completely coherent. Something about being kicked in the head by a mutant tri-hoofed fergilla. "But I speak truth, beloved. It is not safe for you to be here. The battle could be joined at any moment, and—"

"And you aren't flying yet, so I still have my chance." Georgia eased toward Fari, reached out, and stroked his shoulders. "If Krysta calls you to go, I'll jump ship and head to Camford, I swear. So, will you listen now?"

Fari nodded.

At that, Georgia leaned in, stood on her tiptoes and kissed him, slow and long. The feel of his warm lips, his rough, exploring tongue—what would she do without these things? He smelled like *man*. Salt, leather, sweat—all man. And his shoulder muscles thrilled her each time they flexed beneath her palms.

By the time the kiss ended, Fari's cock was a rock stiff against her belly, and his eyes were closed.

"I love you," she murmured, brushing her lips across his stubbled cheeks. "When you get back, I want to marry you, by whatever custom you choose."

"You are serious?" Fari's eyes snapped open.

Georgia nodded. "I would never joke about something so important."

Fari pulled her closer, joining their bodies in full embrace. Georgia lost herself in his smell, the feel of his hard body beneath his tunic and breeches. Arda's fragrant, sensual air caressed her just as her lover's hands, and for a moment, Georgia felt overwhelmed by her new reality. This planet, her psi-powers, her new family, her new home. She had never felt so involved, such a live and integral part of…of everything.

She belonged on Arda, and she belonged in Fari's loving arms.

"I love you with my whole heart, my whole mind, shanna." His baritone whisper in her ear gave Georgia sweet chills. "But now, I want you to go. I need to know you have reached Camford safely."

Georgia slipped her hand into his breeches and grabbed his rigid cock. "A few more minutes, *sha*."

Fari's every muscle seemed to vibrate when Georgia used the Ardani term for soul's mate. Passion flared in his eyes, and Georgia knew remnants of the mating fervor had captured him once more.

Her pussy ached for him, and her own thoughts turned dizzy as she tugged his shirt up so their *pa* marks could touch.

Maybe the mating fervor had snuck up on her, too.

Georgia kept one hand on Fari's cock, threw her free arm around his neck, and gave him a lip-crushing kiss. His tongue drove into her mouth, finding hers even as their *pa* crackled and blended. She squeezed the hot, hard flesh in her hand, and Fari groaned. Letting go her psi-barriers, Georgia felt the raging wilderness of her lover's mind. She also sensed Krysta's presence, and Elise's, and another— no doubt Ki. So distant, but no less engaged.

They were worried.

Intrigued.

And excited.

Hurry, Elise urged. *We don't have much time, and this could be the only time.*

With a shock, Georgia processed her meaning. The battle was brewing. Anything could happen. This might be the one time the Tul'Mar's newly constructed family could join sexually. Fear, thrill, distress, and an overwhelming urgency gripped Georgia's being.

She had a mental image of Elise pinching her own nipples, stroking her own clit. In her mind's eye, Krysta was doing the same, using one of the control levers in her speeder as a makeshift dildo. Even Ki, phantom image though he was, had his big prick out, pumping it slowly.

The sensation of watching, of being watched, pushed Georgia to a level of frenzy she had never known.

Fari lifted her like a doll and laid her back against the edge of the observation nest. He bent over her and claimed a nipple in his teeth, nibbling, sucking, biting all at once. Georgia moaned and wrapped her legs around his hips.

Yessss... Elise's pleasure whispered through Georgia's sex-sated brain. Elise was lying in a big bed, stroking her clit fast and hard.

Krysta fucked herself with the speeder's control lever, moving up and down, eyes closed. Her moans floated through the psi-link like ripples on a pond.

Ki's grunts seemed like exclamation points, and Georgia thought she could hear his hand sliding up and down his prick with increasing speed.

She gripped Fari's shoulders hard and pressed her hot pussy against his cock. Only the fabric of his breeches separated her from paradise. "Fuck me," she begged. "I need you inside me."

Fari hunched against her, teasing, first kissing her lips and then her nipples.

Georgia's groans were joined by three others through the link. The combined pleasure, excitement, anticipation—it was enough to make Georgia's mind an expanding balloon.

And then Fari stepped back and turned her around, so that she gripped and bent over the smooth, *pa*-coated edge of the observation nest. Her breasts dangled, brushing the cool metal as she heard the rustle of Fari dropping his pants behind her.

The tip of his cock teased her slick pussy from behind, nudging until she spread her legs. Shocks ran through Georgia, from her toes to the ends of her pebbled nipples. Her own pleasure, and Elise's, and Krysta's, as they enjoyed small orgasms, building for bigger and bigger climaxes. Ki was holding back, increasing the tension more and more.

Georgia's fingers curled on the rounded edge of the nest. It seemed like all of Arda stretched before her. Lake and field and forest. Her pussy throbbed, waiting for penetration. She felt like she would scream if Fari didn't enter deep and hard, right that second.

He teased her with another nudge.

Georgia did scream. She spread her legs wider, feeling *pa*-coated wood hum against her belly and breasts. Fari gripped her hips and slipped the tip of his cock into her pulsing opening.

More moans of frustration and pleasure echoed in Georgia's mind.

"That's it, damn it." She groaned and thrust herself backward, taking more of his length. "Fuck me before I get my swords and kill you!"

Fari pushed her forward, back against the edge of the nest, and with a blistering yell, he thrust deep. So, so deep. Heat blazed through Georgia as she screamed again. Fari's weight pinned her against the nest wall. He held her there for a long moment, moving his cock inside her, grinding his balls against her wet outer lips. His *pa* sizzled along the top of her ass.

"Shanna," Fari murmured. "I could hold you here forever."

Georgia couldn't speak. The walls of her pussy contracted, squeezing tight against his shaft as he slowly, ever so slowly slid back, then slipped deep again.

Elise had another orgasm. Krysta was pounding herself on the smooth metal and rubber of her speeder control. Ki's hand moved at a furious pace, beating his prick with no mercy.

Once more, Georgia's thoughts swirled into near-madness. Fari's mind went with her. He braced his hands on either side of her, holding her fast against the nest wall, and drove his cock into her pussy with fierce abandon.

"Oh, God. Yes. Please, fuck me like that." Georgia held on tight to the edge, feeling her body rock into the soft cushion of *pa* on the wood. Her legs were splayed wide, and only Fari's rock-solid arms kept her from pitching out of the nest each time he slammed into her.

A creaking and groaning rose around them, and somewhere in the dim recesses of Georgia's rational thoughts, she processed that the ship was moving. Lurching. Starting to drift over the burned docks at the river's edge.

And yet every nerve in her body was on fire. If she could have sucked Fari into the center of her body, she would have. "Do it. Yeah." She wiggled her ass as he plumbed her deeper, harder, faster.

Georgia had never been fucked like this, even on the island. Fari's cock felt like sun-forged steel, turning her pussy to a molten pool of want. Of need.

His breath whistled in frayed huffs.

Georgia gasped with each thrust. He filled her up. He jammed her to capacity, all the while scrubbing his *pa* on her ass, pressing her *pa* into *Lorelei*'s coated boards. Orgasm built in her groin like slow-lit gunpowder, scorching a path through her belly, up into her chest, to her nipples, her shoulders, her fingers.

Elise came with a body-rocking psi-scream, and Ki shot his load at the same moment. Seconds later, Krysta's mental shouts of pleasure filled the link.

And then, yelling, watching the ground move below as the ship sailed over the fields of Camford, Georgia came harder than she'd ever come in her life. Her senses reeled. Her brain turned off and on like a flickering neon bulb.

Her pussy gripped Fari's cock like jaws, and he bellowed as he blew his seed deep into her channel.

Tears of release flooded Georgia's cheeks as she moved her ass against Fari's tight groin, getting all she could of her lover before he had to let her go.

The castle loomed before *Lorelei*, the stone and mortar fortress a sobering reminder of reality. The defense of home and hearth. The danger in orbit above them.

A few staff ran to and fro below the sleek frigate. Some looked up to see Georgia, now standing, still impaled on Fari's cock.

She didn't care.

Let them look and wish they could fuck something so good, so perfect.

Fari nuzzled her neck, and bit by bit, the psi-link that had joined them with Ki, Elise, and Krysta melted away.

I must go, shanna.

I know. Georgia's tears turned hot and bitter. *Promise me you'll come back.*

Fari hesitated, then hugged her tight, his strong arms crisscrossing her belly. The heat of his breath warmed her ear, and he whispered, "I promise."

Chapter 16

Georgia barely remembered climbing down *Lorelei's* riggings and being helped to the ground by castle staff not already in castle defense positions. Someone gave her a tunic and breeches, and she pulled them on numbly.

The silver frigate holding the love of her life took on a few spare hands, then floated, ghost-like, back over the fields and out of sight.

Fari didn't even lean out of the observation nest to wave goodbye.

Maybe that was bad luck on Arda, or something.

Georgia bit her lip.

No bad luck. No ill omens. No. Nothing but good energy. Positive energy.

The Outlander ships had yet to move out of orbit formation, but as grief cleared Georgia's mind, she sensed danger drifting high overhead, like ominous thunderclouds. Fari's thoughts were closed to her now, as were Ki's, and Krysta's. They would be concentrating on anticipation, offensives, and counteroffensives. And if Georgia understood what she had been told, Ki and the Fleet were still hours away. Too far for real assistance if the bandits attacked.

It would be up to the Home Guard—and Fari on the *Lorelei.*

As Georgia made her way into the nearly-deserted castle, she wondered why the Outlanders *didn't* strike. If they moved now, they had a chance to decimate Arda's basic defenses.

And yet they just hung there.

Taunting? Daring?

Waiting...but for what?

Where are you? Elise's distressed psi-cry penetrated Georgia's nervous musings.

Georgia tensed immediately. Fatigue left her in a rush, replaced by an urgent need to hurry to her cousin. Something was wrong. Elise's thoughts felt like a knife digging into bare flesh.

The maze of Camford's halls didn't faze Georgia. Elise's mental sobs drew her down halls and stairways like a giant magnet. Deeper and deeper into the castle. To its center. To its heart.

Long *pa*-drenched halls stretched before her, darker and darker silver as she went. The thickening stone and higher *pa* content reminded Georgia of a bomb shelter—and that made some weird sort of sense.

Of course Camford's depths would be fortified. It *was* a castle, a fort, right? The extra *pa* probably made it harder for stray psi-signals to get in or out—yet strengthened psi abilities if you knew how to channel the energy.

Strategic command center. Nerve center. All sorts of silly military jargon cluttered Georgia's thoughts.

Hey! Georgia! Are you hurrying? Please be hurrying.

Coming. She took a sharp left, and immediately knew she had reached her destination as she entered a rounded chamber with four doors at points she figured for due north, south, east, and west.

Elise's calls emanated from the south, and Georgia hurried to the door. It wasn't locked.

"Help me," her cousin moaned as Georgia rushed inside—and nearly freaked out completely.

Someone had moved her paintings in here and hung them on the walls. All of them, finished and unfinished. Someone had realized the importance—that losing the paintings would feel like a loss of life to Georgia.

Fari? Elise? Or maybe Krysta. It does have a Krysta touch to it.

A bluish, unnatural light bathed the small, rounded and windowless room. A few torches flickered from silver brackets on the rock walls, and tapestries hung like curtains on the stone between Georgia's pictures. In a corner, she saw swords—Elise's, and hers. Both ruby blades. Someone must have brought them, presumably in case they were needed. Furnishings were sparse—a desk, a chair, and one big four-poster bed. Where Elise lay dressed in a tunic and shorts, legs spread, hands on her enormous belly.

Obviously in labor.

"Oh...my...God." Georgia rubbed her throat as if forcing the words to come. "Where are the priests? Does this place have a midwife?"

"Akad—" Elise began, then let loose with a long, frantic moan.

Georgia's mind filled in the rest. "He's gone with the rear Guard to meet the Fleet. Damn it. And the rest of the priests are flying with the front and main guard. And you—you weren't supposed to have sex! Shit!"

Elise wailed, and Georgia ran to the bed, climbed on, and held her cousin's head in her lap. She had no idea what to do, but she couldn't stand to see Elise in such pain.

Boil water. Get clean towels. They do that on old T.V. shows, right? Georgia stroked Elise's hair. "Shit! Shit! Shit! When did this start?"

Elise panted for a few seconds, then managed to squeak, "Right after I—uh—we—came."

"Why did you do that? You knew better!"

"Because I was afraid we wouldn't—"

"Shut up. Don't say anything negative. Shit." Georgia started panting with Elise, in spite of her best effort not to.

"Aaaaaaah, damn, I have to push!" Elise squirmed against Georgia and shoved against the top of her belly.

"Wait! Don't!" Georgia got up and turned in circles trying to think. *Wait. Don't. Like that'll stop everything. I'm such a dumbass. Okay, no water here to boil, and I'm not leaving her. What else have I seen on T.V.? Come on, come on. I've read every damn edition of* Our Bodies, Ourselves.

Elise groaned and pushed on her belly again.

Holding her breath to suffocate the freak-out, Georgia chose a course of action. Lightning-fast, she climbed back on the bed, grabbed the pillows Elise wasn't using, and crammed them under Elise's backside. Then she slid Elise's shorts off and gently spread her legs.

Everything looked oddly wide and expanded.

Another spasm gripped Elise, and this time she screamed.

"It's okay. Push, I guess. I—oh, shit." Georgia's heart fluttered as she saw what appeared to be a dark thatch of hair in thin silver coating pushing its way out of Elise.

It is hair. It's a head! The baby's crowning!

"Ilya!" Elise yelled her daughter's name and pushed, just as Georgia managed to slip her hands under the baby's emerging neck.

"She's coming." Georgia's voice cracked. Her throat felt as dry summer dirt. "Push some more! I think."

Elise pushed.

Ilya seemed stuck in place. Her teeny face was still and puckered inside her silver veil, and her color went from blood to beet to almost purple.

"Gaaaaaahhh!" Elise wriggled on the pillows and bore down on her belly.

Panicked, Georgia reached inside Elise as best she could, feeling Ilya's little shoulders. An inch at a time, she turned the baby just a bit, just enough for one shoulder to pop free.

Elise let out a huge breath.

Georgia felt like she was going to faint. For a second she just sat there, supporting Ilya, not sure what came next—until Elise answered all questions.

With a stone-cracking screech, Elise sat up, shoving so hard on her belly Georgia wondered if she'd push the flesh right off.

Seconds later, Ilya literally slipped into Georgia's hands.

"There's a baby. In my hands. I mean—you did it!" Giddy relief seized Georgia. "She's here! Ilya's here!"

And then Georgia's mind registered three more things.

Elise had passed out, and she was bleeding badly.

Ilya was still inside a silver sac, as still and silent as an unhatched chick.

And there was a unnaturally huge man standing in the room, right next to the bed, staring at all three of them.

* * * * *

Fari Tul'Mar stood on the aft deck of *Lorelei*, under light tree cover near the ruined building yards. In the back of his mind, he felt a stir. Fear, from Georgia. Distress, from Elise. And something else, something different—all muffled by the defense-endowed thick *pa* around the war room. But the Sailkeeper knew he had to shut out the distractions.

If his shanna faced real danger, she would get the message through to him. Of that, he felt certain. He had only to think of the way she nearly blew a hole in his brain when she was angry in the observation nest—yes. Georgia was more than capable of sending an emergency psi-call through the heavy *pa*. She would probably blast down the mental barriers of the entire Fleet if she did, too.

Brother. Ki's command tone overrode all other thought. *Our sensors indicate —*

The Outlander ships are moving! Krysta's psi-shout finished the Sailmaster's sentence.

Hold position, Fari instructed his sister. *Time, Ki. How long until you reach us?*

Two stellar hours. One and a half if fortune favors.

May the universe hear our plea. Fari gripped the hilt of his barbed sword. His nostrils flared as his eyes searched the sky.

Watching.

Waiting.

Home Guard at the ready? Came Krysta's authoritative call to arms.

Aye, Captain! answered hundreds of star sailors on dozens of Home Guard speeders.

Keep it simple. Keep it clean. Krysta's battle-lust spattered her thoughts like drops of blood. *Close the net. For Arda! Close the net!*

Chapter 17

He has yellow eyes. Tiger eyes. Georgia held Ilya like a silver-swathed Ming vase between Elise's pale legs and gaped at the man in the room.

Why hadn't she sensed his thoughts when he entered? Was he shielding that well? Her swords...could she reach them and somehow keep hold of the baby?

"Look, whoever you are. I've got trouble here." Georgia held up Ilya. "I think something's wrong."

The intruder stood taller than Fari or even Ki, dressed in what looked like deerskin breeches and a leather-laced deerskin shirt. His onyx hair was pulled back severely and smoothly, clasped behind his head. The sharp angles of his face and his deep, deep brown skin reminded Georgia of Native Americans. Only she was on Arda, not Earth. And this stranger had his hand on the hilt of what looked like a holstered double-bladed axe.

His eyes drifted around the room, taking in Georgia's paintings. These clearly fascinated him.

"*Tu?*" he asked, pointing at an unfinished image of Fari, one that captured the warrior's light and dark sides.

"Yes. I painted those. And, damn! I don't have time for this!" Georgia turned her attention back to Ilya. "Help me or get fucked. I don't care."

The tiny girl moved, but the sac seemed to be constricting her. Was it suffocating her, too? Georgia plucked at it, trying to rip it open.

From the corner of her eye, she watched the man. As he stared at them, his expression shifted from cruel hunger to grim resignation, and finally to outright annoyance. Or anger. Georgia couldn't tell.

She glanced at Elise. Her cousin had turned the color of day-old dough. The damn sac around the baby wouldn't give, either. Georgia considered using her teeth.

Ilya stopped moving.

"*Baska,*" Tiger-Eyes spat.

"Baska off, asshole!" Georgia was so confused and upset she wanted to throw up. There had to be a way to get Ilya out of the friggin' silver bag!

The stranger looked slightly surprised, and then his lips quirked into a smile. Or it might have been a snarl. He rolled his freaky eyes, and his hand left his weapon. He gestured to Elise.

"*Da domna, el et sang maldro.*" He stared at Georgia, as if waiting for some response.

Georgia tried to ignore him, biting at the birth sac. The jerk's language sounded like Ardani, but neither the archaic or newer version she had come to know. She tried to communicate mind to mind to see if she could gain a quick understanding of his dialect, but when she reached for the man's thoughts, she felt like she was trying to link with a flat rock.

Shivering, Georgia realized that the only other time she felt a similar sensation was in the forest, the day two of Darkyn Weil's personal guards had attacked her.

"*Da Domna, el et sang. Maldro! Maldro!*" This time, Tiger-Eyes looked at her like she was stupid. "*Vit. Vit!*" He made a flicking motion with his fingers.

This is the Twilight Zone, Georgia thought, now desperate. In absolute panic. She was sure Ilya was dying. Maybe the swords in the corner. Yes. One of them might rip the silver shit away from the baby.

She started toward them, but just then, the man heaved a great sigh, strode forward, and got onto the bed beside Georgia and Elise.

"Oh, now, wait one minute," Georgia began, but before she could figure out how to react, the man snatched Ilya from her hands.

"No you don't!" Georgia rocked back on her knees and drew back her fist to whop his head, but the man ignored her. His intense yellow eyes fixed only on Ilya, and his huge brown fingers tore open the spidery silver sac as if it were paper. Georgia saw a flash of brighter silver, the baby's *pa* mark, she realized. Whorls covered Ilya's chest, tummy, and neck, forming what looked like the swirls of a tornado.

After discarding the sac he ripped away, Tiger-Eyes worked at the baby's nose and mouth, clearing birth's debris.

Georgia held back on hitting him.

"Are you a priest?"

Still, the man ignored her. He raised the baby, covered her tiny mouth and nose with his own mouth, and blew hard. Once. Twice.

As Georgia watched, stunned, the infant's feet kicked. Her teeny hands curled. The weird man drew back, and Ilya turned a fine shade of strawberry. She opened her little lips, and she wailed at the top of her impressive baby lungs.

"You—I—thank you!" Georgia clapped her hands together just as Tiger-Eyes thrust the baby toward her. Off guard, all Georgia could do was catch Ilya in a basket hold, like a running back accepting a handoff.

The baby stopped crying almost immediately, snuggled into the crook of Georgia's arm, and seemed content.

The intruder gestured for Georgia to get off the bed. The moment she complied, he focused his attentions on Elise. He examined the bleeding with his eyes, then held his hands inches above her belly, muttering to himself. His expression shifted again, and this time, Georgia thought he looked nervous. Maybe afraid. She stood between the big bed and the door, wishing Akad would come running in to save the day.

This is not good.

At her tense thought, Ilya reacted with whimpers and whining.

Tiger-Eyes shook his head and sighed. "*Baska.*"

"You *are* a priest, right?" Georgia asked more to convince herself than to get a response from the stranger. "Can you help her?"

True to form, the man ignored Georgia.

He gently removed the pillows from beneath Elise and threw them on the floor. Georgia cradled Ilya and watched, too stunned to move, as Tiger-Eyes straddled Elise at the knees and unlaced his leather tunic to his midsection. He had a *pa* mark, yes, in a shape similar to the double axe he wore at his hip—but in the center, where imaginary blades met imaginary hilt, a black stone glistened.

Georgia chilled to her marrow. *Just like my attackers in the woods. They had those stones, but theirs were dull and lifeless compared to this.*

She realized the stone was not some artifice or piercing—no. This stone *grew* where it lay, a part of the man's flesh and *pa*.

As if hearing Georgia, the man ran his fingers across his stone as he stared at Elise. The stone glimmered like a dark diamond.

"*Anno,*" he intoned, keeping one hand over his body-stone and one hand over Elise's stomach. "*Anno san dranon. Anno. Anno san sanguo. Anno...*"

The hypnotic timbre and rhythm quickly made Georgia's eyelids droop. Even Ilya fell asleep in seconds, listening to the strange priest work his spell.

"*Anno san dranon. Anno. Anno san anguo. Anno. Anno san dranon...*"

Tiger-Eyes rocked back and forth, chanting, while Georgia fought to stay awake. After a while, she heard nothing but the drumming of the man's voice.

Then, without warning, the man clapped his hands together. "*Dora, Elise Tul'Mar. Dora!*"

Georgia snapped awake. *Dora.* She knew that word. It was archaic Ardani for "hold," as in "hold on," only it came from the lesser-known high speech, now considered extinct. A few words, like *dora*, had survived through ceremonial use. With sufficient strength behind the speaker, it would constitute an irresistible psi-command.

Had this man been speaking the old high speech of Arda all along?

If so, why wouldn't he communicate with her mind-to-mind, so she could understand him?

He obviously knew who Elise was—but then most citizens did. And yet, that stone in his abdomen.

Are all people with the stones Outlanders?

Elise's skin began to regain some of its natural luster and pinkness. She stirred beneath the man, eyelids fluttering, then grew still. Georgia heard the welcome, easy sound of sleep-breathing, and her extra senses told her Elise's crisis had passed.

Thank the universe.

Tiger-Eyes stopped his ministrations, climbed off Elise, and slid from the bed to face Georgia. Instinctively, she pulled Ilya closer, even though she believed the man had saved the baby's life—and Elise's.

Once more, the stranger's features hardened. His hand drifted to the hilt of his axe, and his eyes narrowed. Inside those odd yellow orbs, warmth seemed to war with a bleak coldness, and Georgia didn't like the looks of the battle.

She held her ground, though. There was nowhere to run, with him standing between her and the door. In the corner, on the other side of the bed, Georgia's own swords waited. She could never get to them in time, if this guy decided to get rough.

But why would he spill blood after spending so much time and energy saving lives?

Ilya fidgeted and started to cry.

Georgia told herself she should put the infant down, out of the fray, if there was to be a fray. Her eyes darted around the room.

Where? On the bed next to Elise? On the floor beneath the bed? Was there any safe place?

Maybe the best defense is a good offense.

"What do you want?" Georgia demanded, giving Tiger-Eyes the toughest scowl she could muster with a wailing newborn in her arms.

The man's face darkened—and two more giants lumbered into the bedroom.

Georgia's chest tightened. She knew them immediately. The thugs who attacked her in the forest, before she went to Ammon Island with Fari. *Fari! Ki! Krysta!* She fought a sheer black terror as she backed away, bumping into the bed. *Help. Help us, please!*

Deafening mental silence answered Georgia's psi-call. She had a vague sense of star battles blazing overhead, of Ardani speeders falling out of the sky, of the Fleet rushing toward home at impossible speeds. The images dizzied her. She blocked them out, becoming all too aware of the terrible two who had just entered the room.

They leered at her and drew menacing swords with polished black blades. Frick and Frack, Georgia's numbed mind christened them. Frick winked at the yellow-eyed titan, who stood no more than a foot from Georgia and the howling Ilya.

Tiger-Eyes's inscrutable face turned stony. "*Nado*," he growled.

Frick and Frack gaped at him. "*Da Domna!*" Frack shouted. He pointed at Georgia. "*El et Tul'Mar.*"

"*Nado*," the yellow-eyed man said again, this time slowly, louder, over-enunciating as if his listeners had some mental impairment.

Frick seemed about to explode. He gestured to Elise and the baby in Georgia's arms. "*El ets assi Tul'Mar!*"

Acting on instinct, Georgia snuggled Ilya and inched back. The three men kept arguing in their strange almost-Ardani, paying her little mind.

Emboldened, Georgia walked around the bed, making a show of returning Ilya to Elise. The baby struggled and cried as Georgia nestled her against her sleeping mother.

Just as Georgia eased back from the bed, Tiger-Eyes leaped in front of Frick and Frack, blocking their access to Elise and the newborn. He drew his axe, and Georgia gasped.

The brutal-toothed, double-headed murder weapon was the same startling yellow as the man's eyes. It seemed radiant, like starlight enslaved in metal. Just looking at it made her squint, and she felt nauseated.

On the bed, Elise moaned, and Ilya began a new round of loud crying.

"Nado!" Tiger-Eyes bellowed.

Frick and Frack began to back toward the door. Reluctantly.

Tiger-Eyes brandished his terrifying axe, swiping the air to force them out of the room. *"Alle. Alle!"*

Georgia wasted no time. No matter her urge to puke, this was her only chance. She lunged for the corner, grabbed her ruby blades, and let the scabbards clatter to the floor.

As soon as the two goons left, Tiger-Eyes wheeled on Georgia.

Biting back surges of bile, she burst around the end of the bed, a red sword in each fist. Beneath her tunic, along her neck, across her cheeks, her *pa* crackled, and the ruby blades flickered like fire.

"Get out of here!" she yelled, rushing at the man with the starlight weapon.

Clearly surprised, he stumbled back, slamming into the door facing. He kept his grip on his axe, but barely.

Georgia stopped her charge a few feet away. Her stomach churned from the sight of that freaky yellow blade. She didn't want to fight this guy. She'd lose. But...maybe he'd think she was crazy. Maybe he didn't know what she could or couldn't do with her ruby swords.

Sometimes bluff was everything.

Tiger-Eyes studied her with a curious, then appreciative gaze.

"Come on." Georgia stomped her foot and shook the swords. "You want a piece of me? What are you waiting for?"

The man actually chuckled. "*Ne discute. Nado. Nado.*"

Keeping his free hand raised in a gesture of surrender, he sheathed his bizarre axe.

On the bed, Elise and Ilya quieted. Georgia felt a measure of relief, and her nausea eased.

She did not lower her swords.

Tiger-Eyes now had both hands in the air. He snapped his feet together and offered Georgia a small bow.

Then, without further gesture or comment, he backed out of the room and closed the door behind him.

Georgia dropped her blades, ran forward, and slid the locking bolt into place.

Behind her, Ilya whimpered.

Elise's sleepy voice asked, "What's happening?"

The door rattled. Someone hammered on it, and to Georgia's horror, she felt the wood bow with the force of the blows.

Shouts and curses filled the halls outside.

Georgia put her face in her shaking hands and sobbed.

Chapter 18

Fari Tul'Mar piloted *Lorelei* like a man possessed, easing her around tight turns, through narrow mountain passes, keeping her too low for primitive mechanical detection.

The Outlanders had thus far put up a terrific fight. With a surprising show of force, they broke through the protective net of speeders over Camford, driving ship after ship out of the sky. Oddly, few Ardani craft had been destroyed. The bastards seemed to want to cripple the Home Guard. Keep them at bay.

For what reason?

Fari had no time to ponder the intricacies of Darkyn Weil's insane machinations. He had picked up stranded speeder crews, and *Lorelei* was near at full complement.

Krysta had gathered two more speeders to her hidden location—minor damage to outer rudders, quickly repaired.

The perimeter defenses around Camford, the focus of the Outlander assault, were failing. They had to act now, or soon Weil's ships could land *en masse* on the castle's front lawn.

Fari gripped the hilt of his sword. *Sister.*

I am here, Brother. At the ready.

Any word from the rear Guard?

No. I called them back to help us here. The Fleet has not been sighted, though Ki's psi-assistance grows stronger by the moment.

Fari's gut twisted. And then Krysta's words twisted it more.

Fari, did you...did it seem to you that Georgia called to us a few stellar minutes back? It was faint, but —

We cannot think of that now. Fari's teeth ground together. His gut burned like he'd been stabbed. Mating fervor was no longer an issue. Now he fought a bigger battle. The safety of his world, his people, versus the needs of his shanna. His sweet, sweet beloved.

If something happened to her, he would cut out his own heart.

And yet he could not abandon his post, surrender his planet to an invading force to defend one woman.

By the universe, but he wanted to.

Brother....

Krysta's centering voice brought him back to the moment.

The rear Guard is moving into position. Engage the pincer maneuver. The moment the tide turns, I will drop to ground and go to Georgia and Elise.

Fari nodded as if Krysta stood next to him.

And I will be just behind you — or perhaps leading the way. Pick me up at the building yard as soon as we secure Camford's air space.

He moved to the foredeck, where his crew could see him. Snarling, he grabbed the nearest rigging, leaned near to the ship's edge, and drew his barbed blade.

"For Arda!" the Sailkeeper of Arda shouted, in his mind and aloud.

"For Arda!" roared his fellow warriors.

Lorelei abruptly changed course, driving up, up, up from the trenches where she hid. She burst north over Camford's forest, and Fari knew any Outlander in the range of sight spotted only a long blur of silver.

At the same moment, Krysta's speeders sailed out of cover and moved toward the Outlanders from the west.

The rear Guard, only a handful of speeders but heavily armed and more than battleworthy, dropped out of the eastern stars.

The contingent of surviving Outlander vessels, perhaps twelve in all, scattered in confusion and apparently without a plan.

Fari knew if their captains had been psi-gifted, he would have heard their abject frustration. So close to victory. Now so close to defeat.

Lorelei came scathingly close to a fleeing Outlander ship, a lumbering thing that probably started life as a cargo runner.

With great power of will, Fari held his ship steady, matching the other vessel's speed. Extending the inertial bubble of *Lorelei* around his quarry, he roared boarding instructions to his men.

In his hand, his sword hummed.

Fari bared his teeth.

Damn the Outlanders.

It was time to clear the skies.

Less than one stellar hour later, the Outlanders were in complete disarray. Rogue ships that hadn't been destroyed were forced to ground. A few fled into space, some unfortunate enough to go south, into the waiting arms of Ki Tul'Mar and the unforgiving might of Arda's returning Royal Fleet.

Fari could hear Ki's unkind, hungry laughter through the psi-link.

His brother was taking orbit now, "kicking ass," as Georgia would say.

Georgia. Shanna.

Fari's heart felt squeezed, as if some cruel hand choked away its beat.

Shouting orders and appointing crew members to manage prisoners, see to clean ups, and run patrols for further treachery, Fari took *Lorelei* back to dock and turned her over to his first mate.

There was no sign of Krysta.

Fari cursed. He didn't want to wait. He *couldn't* wait. He had to get to Georgia. *Now.*

Still cursing, he set out for Camford on foot. A nearby speeder quickly picked him up, and he rode the few stellar minutes home in a brooding, anxious silence.

Even as he disembarked at the castle's main gates, Fari combed through different psi-chatter, reaching for Georgia's essence. He could find no indication of her presence. Dread filled him like poisoned water, eating away his insides as he ran up the steps, sword drawn.

Castle staff swirled around him like ants, cleaning, picking up, making way for Home Guard warriors and returning Fleet officers as they came to give report. Light smoke stung his eyes and nose.

Wood and cloth, burned.

There had been a battle in the castle.

Sweat gathered on Fari's neck.

Chairs, tables, paintings, tapestries—hacked to pieces and smoldering.

Even as he neared the war room, the path of destruction did not diminish. It looked like a wall of flame had blazed a path from the castle doors, down the passageway—and straight into the heart of Camford.

Where Georgia had gone, to stay safe with Elise.

"No." Fari kept his blade drawn. He moved at a hard run now, intent on reaching the chamber where Georgia should be.

If she were injured, he would go immediately to find the fergilla who harmed her. If she were—he couldn't even think it—but if his shanna had not survived this strange fire, Fari would kill those responsible and simply fall on his blade's barbs and have done with it. He would not—could not—live without his beloved.

A crowd of staff and warriors clustered around the inner chamber's door.

"Move aside," Fari demanded.

They parted like the sea, but chatter flailed him as he rushed toward the closed door of the Captain's quarters.

"The *Lorelei*…"

"The fire-haired one, Georgia…"

"She saved them…"

"Heard she used her blades…"

"But what burned the halls? It had to be…"

Blocking out all words, all psi-babble, Fari hurtled through the chamber door. If it had been locked, he likely would have walked through it, as if it were no more than papyrus.

Georgia's two ruby blades lay on the floor.

The chamber's bed was coated in blood.

No!

A shout of rage and pain rose from Fari's core. His fingers strangled his sword hilt as he raised the weapon, turned—and came face to face with his brother.

Ki Tul'Mar was grinning like a drunken youngling. In his arms lay a swaddled bundle, and from that bundle, a tiny pink fist jabbed into the air. Elise leaned against his arm, looking exhausted, but otherwise hale.

Hanging on Ki's other arm—

"Georgia." Fari dropped his sword. "Shanna!"

And then he was holding her, reveling in her softness, drinking in her woman's scent of wild berries.

"My daughter," Ki was saying, as if from some other universe or dimension. "Ilya has arrived. My beautiful daughter!"

Sha. Georgia's thoughts reached out and took hold of Fari's. *I love you.*

Fari's cock stiffened to stone. He picked Georgia up, intending to carry her back to his bedchamber and straight to the bath basin.

Already he could imagine her skilled hands, soaping him from head to toe. How sweet her nipples would taste in his eager mouth. He wanted to spread her legs and fuck her in the water. It would feel like flying.

She nuzzled his neck, conveying her approval—and the ache of her pussy. *I want you inside me. I want you so much!*

Fari turned to leave the room, but a wounded warrior stumbled in, bleeding from his neck and arm, and fell on the floor.

The soldier was Kolot, Krysta Tul'Mar's second in command.

Georgia stiffened in Fari's embrace, and he set her gently back on her feet.

Ki handed his daughter back to Elise and shouted for healers.

Two priests hurried in and knelt by the injured man. Neither was Akad, and for some reason, this increased Fari's growing disquiet.

"Where is our sister?" he asked in the calmest voice he could muster.

Ki's soft growl added emphasis, as did Georgia and Elise's collective intake of breath.

The priests worked furiously to stem Kolot's bleeding, but they were obviously losing at the effort.

A new beast of anger roared in Fari's mind and heart as he guessed the truth.

Darkyn Weil's strange plans no longer seemed strange.

Dastardly. Infuriatingly cunning.

And the last plans the Outlander bastard would ever have the pleasure of pulling together.

Fari's own words, spoken just after the attack on the shipyard, came back to barb his heart.

If Weil wanted a Tul'Mar, he would have sent a small army...

Kolot reached out a feeble hand and gripped one of the healers by the robes.

"Taken," he gasped. "Krysta...Outlanders...they took her."

And then his eyes closed, and he spoke no more.

Chapter 19

"What are we going to do?" Georgia followed Fari and Ki into the war room, too exhausted to be strong. Too tired to think clearly. "How will we get her back?"

All vestiges of desire and triumph had been wiped clear by the knowledge of Krysta's kidnapping. The events of the day had left Georgia irritable and frightened beyond measure. Whatever happened after Tiger-Eyes left that chamber, it had been horrible. All the banging on the door. All the yelling. And the halls of Camford were scorched bare, like some fire tornado had tried to spin its way into the castle's heart—or out of it.

And then worrying about Fari, and the dead soldier— thank God the priests had taken Elise back to her own chambers with Ilya.

Two less people to worry about, at least for the next five seconds.

Fari hadn't spoken a word to Georgia since he abandoned their bath plans and put her down. His handsome face radiated rage, and his thoughts remained a closed subject. Ki's narrowed black eyes communicated plenty, though.

Focus. Desperation. Hope, and yet…hopelessness.

"You should leave us." Ki tapped controls on the war room's single black table, and star maps sprang into view—on the table, the walls, the ceiling. The room's intense, thick *pa* coating gave Georgia a drugged feeling. The whole place suddenly felt like a shadowy tomb.

She became aware of the sour sweat and battle stench emanating from Fari and Ki. That odor, mingled with the stink of burned wood, made her eyes water. Still, she folded her arms and insisted, "I want to help."

"My brother asked you to leave." Fari's cold voice shocked and chilled Georgia. "We must concentrate, or Krysta's life could be forfeit."

"I don't think so." Georgia shook her head, smarting from Fari's brush-off. "If the Outlanders had wanted to kill people, they would have killed us."

Fari cut her a sharp glance. "What are you saying?"

"The man I told you about, Ki." Georgia addressed the Sailmaster, hoping for a more logical response. "The one who saved Elise and Ilya, then fought off those two goons. I'm sure he was an Outlander, maybe a captain or some other leader, like I said."

"They attacked us to take Tul'Mar hostages." Fari gazed through Georgia, keeping his attention on the star charts. "Why would they leave you untouched? Likely some low-bred fools who did not realize their boon. You *were* in the military chambers, after all."

Georgia felt heat rise to her cheeks. Fifteen minutes ago, this guy had been ready to carry her off to a relaxing bath, fuck her for hours, marry her, then fuck her for days. Now he talked to her like she was a brainless schoolgirl.

What was wrong with him? His expression was so strange. A cross between fear, defeat—and other things Georgia knew only too well. Self-doubt. Old pain.

Warning flutters in her belly told her Fari had gone to some other place. Some other time. Somewhere awful he hadn't told her about—even though she'd told him about Chuck, the rape...

Bastard.

Choking back anger, she pressed ahead, trying to reason with him. "The man spoke archaic Ardani, only it was the high speech Krysta and Akad told me about and showed me in books. He had no telepathic skills. And, he had a shiny black stone in his skin." She pointed to the center of her stomach. "Right here."

Ki straightened. Even in the room's odd darkness, Georgia could see the flush of rage claiming his face. "Outlander. Yes, he was, as you suspected. The scum."

"Two of them were scum." Georgia kept her eyes away from Fari. "The ones he fought off. But *that* Outlander made Ilya breathe and stopped Elise's bleeding."

"So he could take more Tul'Mar hostages," Fari grumbled. "Or slaughter more Tul'Mar victims."

Georgia groaned. "No! That's what I'm trying to tell you. He could have killed all three of us, or taken us at any time. That's what Frick and Frack—I mean, the two goons—wanted to do, but the man who helped us wouldn't let them. I think he kept fighting in the hall, after I closed the door. Until the fire or whatever happened."

For a time, the brothers fell silent. Georgia suspected they were sharing a private psi-conversation, but she didn't try to eavesdrop. Instead, she studied the myriad of star charts, trying to figure out where Arda was in the diagrams.

It was Fari who broke the silence. "We appreciate what you have told us. Please, go to Elise now, and let us plan how to get Krysta back."

"I want to help with the plan." Georgia heard the sharp bite in her tone. "I'm not stupid. Maybe I can think of something you'd miss."

"On Arda, this is usually a warrior's work," Ki explained, sounding too nice.

"Don't pull this warrior's work shit on me," Georgia snapped. "I'm the one who drew swords on that yellow-eyed bastard when I thought he might hurt us. I'm the one—"

Fari held up one hand. "What did you say?"

"I said I'm the one who was ready to fight Tiger-Eyes for Elise and Ilya. If that doesn't make me a warrior, I don't know what does."

"*He* was here!" Fari turned and grabbed Ki by the shoulders. "Damn the stars! Even as I fought—Darkyn Weil—" and the rest degenerated into strings of curses.

"W-Weil? No." Georgia felt sick again. Like she had when she first saw the stranger's—Weil's—yellow-bladed axe.

Fari's outburst masked a powerful misery. It all but filled the room as Ki grappled with him to calm him down. Georgia wanted nothing more than to go to Fari, but better sense held her in check. He suddenly seemed alien to her, even more alien than Weil.

What churned inside him?

Why hadn't Fari shared this pain with her?

Damn. Self-recrimination nudged out more personal concerns as the totality of the situation came home to Georgia. *Maybe he's mad because I had the Outlander chief at sword-point and let him go!*

But in truth, what she had done was her best, defending Elise and Ilya. They had survived until Fari returned. Wasn't that worth something?

Stop! Fari's blinding psi-response hit Georgia like a slap. *For your life, and the life of Elise and Ki's heir, I am grateful. But in other matters, I have made a grave error.*

"What's with you?" Tears pushed through Georgia's eyes, threatening to spill. "You're mad about so much all of a sudden. Not just Krysta. Not just me. What is it? I'm your lover. Your fiancé. I'm supposed to be your wife soon. Talk to me!"

Fari made a sudden move toward her, but Ki caught his brother around the neck. "This is wrong, Brother. The past sits heavily with you this day."

Fari made no effort to struggle with Ki, who had the clear advantage. Instead, he focused his thoughts on Georgia.

I cannot protect you. That much is obvious. Go to your cousin, to the family you can trust and treasure. As for me, for us — I was mistaken. A good fuck or two or ten does not make a soul's mate. We were not meant for each other. We will not be joined.

Pain crushed Georgia's chest, and she moved her hand to her heart. Maybe if she pressed it tight inside, it wouldn't fall out and break.

Now, get out of here, Georgia Steel, Fari continued. *Get away from me before real harm befalls you.*

Do not listen to him! Ki's psi-voice intruded, but Georgia couldn't follow Ki's suggestions. *He is not fit for decisions now. The pain is too great.*

Shrugging off Ki's pleas, Georgia stumbled and fumbled her way to the war room door, feeling attacked and left for dead inside. She barely knew when she was out of the room, or where she went, or how she got there.

Elise…asleep with her new baby, bathed in the light of her husband's love—something Georgia couldn't bear to see, at least not this moment.

Krysta…kidnapped.

Fari…the man she thought she loved, the man she believed loved her as well, turning on her and showing his true self.

Georgia had never felt so betrayed, so hurt, or so lost.

Or so completely confused.

The castle walls constricted her, and she had to get out. Flee. Go somewhere. Anywhere but here. Arda was a big planet, right? And if she found a speeder, she could travel. To an OrTan slaver skull, if she chose.

Fucking. Obviously what she was good for. Why not? What did it matter?

The curtains around her thoughts closed like iron, and she latched them shut. Enough of this psi-bullshit. It didn't matter. Psi-talk just gave an illusion of knowing someone. It just made it easier to get sucked in at a deeper level, and *really* fucked.

Somehow Georgia made her way to the stables and found Lia. The Chimera's fetching yellow hide glowed, and Georgia had a hard time not thinking about Darkyn Weil's unnatural blades.

Still, she mounted without tack or bridle. Daring something that only Krysta did, Georgia reached to her animal's mind.

Away from here. Her instructions were clear, focused. *Take me someplace where no Tul'Mars will trouble me.*

Stable hands scattered as the great Chimera wheeled around and bolted under Georgia's imperative.

The last sight anyone had of the Sailkeeper's former woman was as a blaze of yellow hide, red hair, and the flash of silvery hooves.

Chapter 20

"You are twelve kinds of fool." Ki slapped Fari across the face just inside the door of Ki's bedchamber. Fari didn't flinch. Neither did he defend himself.

"You drive your shanna to let go her past, to surrender her old wounds and love you," Ki continued as Elise looked on from the bed, nursing Ilya, "but you — oh, no. *You* refuse to do the same. I cannot believe your conceit! Do you think love and trust flows only one way?"

Fari winced at this. It had been two days since Georgia went missing, and slightly longer since Krysta had been kidnapped. Family losses. Horrid, wrenching losses that could not be reclaimed. And they were his fault, as always.

That is ridiculous, Brother. Even Ki's psi-comments came in growls. "And it is that sort of thinking that may cost you the love of your life — and your sanity. This time, and this time alone, the loss *is* your responsibility. You have driven Georgia away from all of us. How do you think Krysta will feel about this when she returns?"

Krysta. The Outlanders had sent word in the form of a package, addressed in the old high speech and the unmistakable flourishing hand of Darkyn Weil himself:

Your soldier is safe. See that she stays that way. Give us no pursuit, and we will soon discuss the situation. You will know our demands, and if we reach successful compromise, this warrior will be returned to you unharmed.

With the letter came two tokens. A black falcon feather, and Krysta's leather jumpsuit.

It galled Fari. He should have known. How could he have sent his sister blindly into some bizarre Outlander trap? Just as he sent his parents into hostile skies, poorly armed, unaware…

Elise shifted Ilya to her other breast. She had spent so much time crying that her eyes were red-ringed and swollen. "Why didn't Georgia come to me? I don't understand. What did you do to her? Tell me, damn it, or I'll kill you in your sleep. When you least expect it."

This threat, at least, caused Fari a moment's worry— and a moment's levity. He had known Elise's vengeance in the past, aboard *Astoria*, when Ki first found her. Her temper could be less than pleasant.

"I did nothing but call off our marriage," he said in quiet, even tones.

"Why?" Elise sounded incredulous. "Because of Krysta? The kidnapping?"

Fari stiffened. "If I cannot protect those I love, then I must not draw them into danger by pretending I can."

"You're an idiot," Elise snapped. "I have never heard anything so stupid."

Ki positioned himself between Fari and the bed where Elise lay, functioning as a formidable shield against Fari's quickly building rage.

"The time has come for you to cease visiting your ire on others, Brother." Ki's ominous warning carried the imperative of command. "Yourself included. No protector is perfect."

"I should be!" Fari raised both fists and smashed them into Ki's chest, but Ki didn't so much as shudder. "And I *have* searched for Georgia. Her thoughts are closed. The trail ended around Browntown, as if she simply vanished. And yet, I do not think she became an Outlander hostage."

"Well, maybe you're not a total idiot." Elise relented. "Just a perfectionistic *male*. I should have known."

Fari blinked, trying to stem the tide of timeworn images. His mother's smiling face. His father's strong handshake. Their vacation schooner blown to bits before it left Arda's orbit. He choked and coughed to clear his throat, but could not speak.

I will locate Georgia, he said through the family psi-link. *If only to assure her safety as best I can and bring her back here, to you.*

"If Georgia doesn't want to be found, you won't find her." Elise sighed and shifted Ilya once again. "We had too many years of hide-and-seek, running from my aunt, from other kids at school. Running from the fact we were orphans. I know my cousin. She's a master of escape, of running away. She's gone somewhere *you* aren't. Where the Tul'Mar name holds little sway is my guess. And she's plotting."

"Plotting what?" Fari imagined waking to the whistle of two ruby blades as they plunged to eviscerate him. Not that he wouldn't deserve it—but, still.

"Her revenge." Elise shrugged. "Some way to hurt you as much as you hurt her—to show herself she doesn't need you, or any of us. Maybe she set out to find Krysta on her own. Never can tell."

"Perhaps I should scour the outlying cities. The distant countries." Fari's heart felt tortured. Georgia was all he could think of, but his mind told him time and again he wasn't good enough for her. He'd failed her. His lack of vision almost got her killed or taken hostage, like Krysta.

"I will manage the search for our sister," Ki said flatly, and Fari knew the Sailmaster was still annoyed.

Fari tightened his grip on his sword. "Because you think I am not competent. Admit it. After what happened to our parents, I should have never been named Sailkeeper. The damned priest Akad would have done a better job."

"Get out," Ki snarled. "Your self-pity tries me."

Fari drew his barbed blade, feeling a mix of self-hatred and blind anger. "Say it, Brother! I am not fit for my duties. I have never been fit. My foolish lack of awareness resulted in the death of our parents, and now our sister—"

Lightning fast, Ki drew his own diamond blade. Before Fari could react, his brother disarmed him with a smashing basal blow to Fari's sword hilt. The shock traveled Fari's arm, and his fingers turned loose the blade on reflex. There was nothing he could do but drop to the floor, gripping his throbbing wrist.

The point of Ki's blade pushed into his throat. Not far enough to penetrate, but far enough to hold Fari—and his attention—as still as a stone.

"What happened to our parents was tragic." Ki spoke slowly, irate teacher to stubborn pupil. "No one knew—no one could have known—of the advances in OrTan skull cloaking. The lizards had never used it before. And they had never made raids to murder. When you scanned for our parents' passage, the skies *were* clear. You sent them off in good faith."

Fari wanted to argue that his senses should have told him otherwise, but the sword at his throat persuaded him to remain silent—and Ki's words were slowly sinking into his brain.

His focus on the past, it was useless. Worthless for Georgia, for Arda—even for himself. And above all, it was selfish.

"As for Krysta," Ki continued as Fari felt his new revelations at the deepest of levels, "she was a willing participant in a brilliant military tactic. Our one error, and I mean *ours*—yours, mine, Krysta's, the Fleet's, every soldier involved—was to misunderstand Outlander purposes. We cannot always be right, Brother. And in the absence of right, we regroup and try again. "

I understand, Brother. A great, hated weight was lifting from Fari as he spoke, replaced by the enormous pain of realizing how he had betrayed his shanna. *I finally* do *understand.*

Ki started to ease his blade back, but from the bed, Elise shouted, "Stop!"

Both men froze in place.

Tenderly, Elise laid Ilya in the center of the massive bed and climbed down to where the two men stood locked in a semblance of combat. When she approached Fari, it was with an expression anything but tender.

She walked right up on him, then knelt until she was eye to eye with her brother-by marriage. Her ample *pa* blazed with the force of her emotion, and Fari couldn't help but think *Lorelei.*

Childhood stories, cultural memories—a thousand factors fed into his sudden respect for this otherworldly woman before him. Elise, yet not Elise. Something more, something older and powerful beyond reason.

"Ki will search for Krysta. You—you find my cousin." Elise's words sounded low and menacing. "You bring her home to us, and heal the damage you inflicted. I want my Georgia whole and happy, or I will make you miserable for her sadness every day of your life, as long as you live."

"Such threats are not necessary." Fari could not nod lest the point of Ki's sword do the damage it was forged to do. "If I fail to find my shanna, to explain myself and ask her forgiveness, my misery will be greater than any you could inflict."

This seemed to satisfy Elise—and Ki, who withdrew his sword.

Whatever it takes. New determination flowed like a river through the Sailkeeper. *I will bring her back to us.*

Chapter 21

The enclave of priests, a spiritual retreat in Arda's distant southern mountains, had to be one of the most beautiful places Georgia had ever seen. Lia, her Chimera, had followed her requests to this perfect place, presumably because Akad had trained her long ago.

Gothic stone structures literally carved into the jagged mountains. Waterfalls too blue to be called crystalline tumbled down the flower-coated slopes. Paths and bridges, carved and polished to remind Georgia of ivory, stretched like lattice-work, connecting libraries to living quarters to common areas. Everything was verdant, alive, green, and healthy. The air offered scents of blossoms and clean water. Rains fell every day, but only for an hour or two, in the late afternoon.

And still, the home of Akad's order offered Georgia little relief from the aching pain in her chest. It had been a week—no, more like a stellar week—since Fari turned her away. After all they had done. After all she had shared with him. From local gossip, Krysta was still missing. And Akad was nowhere to be found, but his fellow priests tended Georgia emotionally as much as she would allow. As for physically, sexually—no. She wasn't up for that. She wasn't sure she'd ever be up for that again.

A monastery seemed like a safe place, only monasteries on Arda weren't the same as those on Earth. Peaceful, yes. Idyllic, certainly. But, damn. The priests had more sex than Earth's most practiced nymphomaniacs.

They fucked hundreds of willing village women. They fucked each other. Alone, in groups, same-sex, mixed-sex—everywhere Georgia turned, orgies abounded. Even more so now that they were preparing for the Festival of Seasons.

As far as anyone knew, the Festival was still on, would still be held on the grounds of Camford in less than two days' time.

That adventuresome part of Georgia's mind, the part of her that hadn't wanted to be tied down before meeting Fari, sometimes rose and wanted to participate in the monastery's charged sexual atmosphere. She even thought about the Festival, and what that experience might bring her.

What *would* it feel like to be fucked in the ass and pussy all at once? And to have a cock in her mouth, too? And just this morning, watching a village woman fully sated by triple penetration—*plus* a cock in each hand—damn.

No wonder Ardani women were fond of mountain climbing.

How many of these monasteries existed?

There was so much Georgia hadn't dared to think about, much less try. These priests seemed designed for one purpose beyond healing, and that was sexual pleasure. Giving a woman whatever she wanted, however she wanted it.

Her pussy stayed wet from morning 'til night, which wasn't conducive to forgetting about Fari.

This particular morning, she had positioned herself in a gazebo, complete with silken couches for relaxation. Georgia reclined on the first couch, which gave her a good view of the living quarters, and many of the common areas — fields, streams, gardens.

Tons of fucking, too.

There, by a golden statue — two women bent over each other in a classic sixty-nine, licking each other's clits and groaning with the perfect match of their pleasure.

Georgia wanted to drop her psi-barriers and enjoy the women's thoughts, but she didn't dare let down her guard. The last thing she wanted was for Fari, Ki, or even Elise to know where she was.

She needed time. She needed healing.

Closer to Georgia, in one of the gardens of yellow flowers, two priests pleasured a village woman. They licked her breasts and toyed with her pussy, each sliding fingers inside her wet slit at the same time. The woman bucked and moaned, clearly finding bliss.

Georgia was naked, and she had brought an Ardani sex toy with her. One of the priests had given it to her — a little vibrator of sorts, like the penis-hilts of Krysta's saddles. No doubt when she put it in her pussy, it would expand to what she needed. Georgia had decided that even if she couldn't bring herself to fuck somebody other than Fari yet, she could damn sure pleasure herself. Her nipples ached, and she squeezed them, not bothering to stifle her moans of relief.

Yes, that felt good.

Maybe people could see her, too. She liked that thought.

"So, I'm an exhibitionist," she admitted, still rolling her beaded nipples between her fingers. "I like to watch — and be watched."

"Happy to oblige," said a low, sexy voice to her left.

Georgia turned to find two priests settling on the gazebo's railing. They were naked, too, twists of *pa* twinkling on their chests and cocks rock-hard. And then a priest and a woman eased up and settled on the other railing.

As Georgia pinched her nipples, the two priests stared at her hands and her breasts. Thrills rippled through Georgia, making her nipples ache all the more. The men smiled and began to massage their own rigid pricks.

Georgia glanced to the right. The woman and her partner kissed, and the priest slipped his hand down, into the woman's shaved folds. His fingers began a slow massage, right on the woman's aching clit.

Her own clit throbbed, and Georgia reached for it.

"Yes," one of the masturbating priests pleaded, "spread your legs. Let us see."

Georgia complied, opening herself to the scrutiny of her audience. It felt so exciting, so right and so wrong at the same time, to feel the heated gazes of other people trained on her slick, pulsing pussy.

A gasp told Georgia that the couple had grown more active. Indeed, the priest had picked up his partner and impaled her on his impressive cock. He leaned against the railing and lifted her up and down. A slow but perfect pace. When the woman's nipples moved before his face, he captured them and sucked, then let go, and captured them again.

"So good." The woman's eyes were closed, but her partner's eyes remained trained on Georgia's pussy.

Georgia stroked her clit, and the three men watching gave low groans of approval. All she had to do was beckon, and they would fuck her any way she directed.

One in her ass, one in her pussy. She could have the other in her mouth, or press her face into the woman's slit and lick the wet silk until the woman came.

But all Georgia did was rub herself harder, faster. She kept one hand on her nipple, pinching it hard.

In front of her, the priests pumped their hard cocks. The woman yelled as her partner increased the speed and depth of his penetration.

"Damn." Georgia let go her nipple, grabbed the sex toy, and crammed it in her pussy. As she had hoped, it warmed, then began to expand.

"Aah. Aaaaah!" The woman came as the priest fucked her like a wild man. "Sweet universe. Yes. Yes!!"

The sex toy in Georgia's pussy hummed and grew, grew and hummed as she fingered her clit.

Then, as if reading her shielded mind, the three priests and the woman moved to one of the other couches. One priest lay back, his rigid prick high and ready as the woman mounted him and leaned forward. The other priest positioned himself behind her, on his knees, and slipped his ample cock slowly, slowly, into her waiting ass.

"Deeper." She groaned, eyes closed. "Fill me up."

Georgia felt her sex toy begin a rapid in-and-out motion. Her clit felt as big as a plum as she rolled it back and forth.

The third priest offered his cock to the woman's mouth, and she took it in with a grateful moan.

As if choreographed by some master dancer, the three men moved in concert, fucking the woman for her pleasure—and for Georgia's.

"Umm. Ummm." The woman's groans doubled the fire between Georgia's legs.

She wanted the woman to come, and come huge. She wanted to watch the woman's body bow and shudder as all three men came inside her.

The sex toy did its work, pumping in and out of Georgia as she once more pinched her own nipples and stroked her clit.

In front of her, the thrusting became frenzied. The woman rocked and groaned, taking every inch of what the priests offered.

Georgia felt her own dose of frenzy, fucking herself, imagining...

Fari, pounding his cock into her pussy...

Ki, behind her, sinking deep...

The yellow-eyed man in her mouth, purring as he stroked her hair...

Krysta and Elise, licking each other's clits as they watched...

With a soul-wrenching howl, Georgia gave into a blistering orgasm. It shook her heart and her mind, and the images she formed wouldn't turn her loose.

She wanted Fari. She needed him. She didn't think she could live without him. And her family, joining the Ardani way—even Tiger-Eyes, somehow a part of them now that he saved Elise and Ilya.

Georgia jerked the sex toy out of her spent channel and flung it across the gazebo. She turned over and rolled into a ball, sobbing like a child who had lost everything.

Vaguely aware of comforting pats and murmured words from the three priests and their willing concubine,

Georgia let herself drift toward a miserable, troubled sleep.

I'll never have the family I dream about. I'll never have what I want, and I have to do something drastic. Close that door in my heart, once and for all, damn it.

And I know just how to do it.

Chapter 22

The Festival of Seasons day dawned clear under big sun and little sister.

Fari stood at Camford's main gates, fighting a feeling that it was wrong. All wrong. To have the Festival with Krysta and Georgia missing—it seemed like heresy. Or glib disregard.

Even the High Priest Akad had not been found. The denizens of his own order had not heard from the priest since the Outlander battle. He was most certainly dead and his body as yet undiscovered—or Akad had been captured and held hostage with Krysta.

Still, Camford's front and side lawns were hives of activity. Bleachers had been hastily constructed, but Fari knew they were well-designed. Banners flapped over different seating areas, sewn in bright, clean cloth to welcome the tribes and towns who would sit beneath them. Life for the people of Arda had to move on.

The Outlanders would make contact. Ki would do whatever it took to win trust, and then the Fleet would recover Krysta and perhaps Akad.

As for Georgia, Fari was at a complete loss.

His mind and muscles were weary from riding. Town after town, enclave after enclave. He had even started on the monasteries, but so far, no luck. Her absence tore at his soul. He missed her so badly he would walk on his knees to her hiding place, if only she would give him the chance to do so.

Had his shanna left the planet?

Stolen some forgotten vessel and departed the system?

Fari sighed and scrubbed his hand over his stubble. Even that made his heart ache. Georgia had enjoyed the feel of his growing beard in between shaves.

Whatever she has done, wherever she has gone, it is my fault. How could I have been so cruel to her?

And what sort of revenge would she exact?

No matter what it was, Fari knew he deserved it. And he knew one more thing for certain. He had to beat back his inner demons and find a way to apologize to his soul's mate. He had to have her back.

Great giggling and laughter tore Fari's attention from his inner musings.

The first of Arda's unclaimed maidens were arriving, these from the planet's western reaches. They were fair of skin but lightly tanned. Most wore Festival gowns of white and yellow, but a few were already naked and draped in flowers. These girls had started merry-making early, judging by the stumble of their gait and the loudness of their bawdy jokes.

Accompanied by priests of the western orders, the girls were led to one of many large tents to begin preparations.

They would be oiled and covered with blossoms, and pleasured to their heart's content by the priests, by each other—and anyone else they chose to include in the gaiety. At the same time, a group of western warriors rode in on horseback, shouting and whooping even as the maidens disappeared from view.

Today, many would find their soul's mates.

Tonight, many would know the fires of mating fervor, and the endless joys of a shanna's love.

At this moment, Fari could scarce imagine such joy, such abandon.

Only Georgia would satisfy his heart, not to mention his stiff, unrepentant cock.

Where are you, beloved? Will you give me no opportunity to redeem myself?

An image of his parents' exploding schooner filled his mind, and Fari grimaced.

Sometimes, the universe gave no second chances.

* * * * *

By the time big sun and little sister crested in Arda's sapphire sky, most of the contingents had arrived. Many were already being seated.

Fari walked with Elise and Ki, listening to the laughter and the moans of pleasure issuing from tents — and even the observation boxes and bleachers surrounding the presentation area.

Elise was clearly aroused. "This is unbelievable. I'm glad Ilya's back in the nursery. I wouldn't want her to see her mom so horny."

Ki pulled Elise close to him, draping an arm around her shoulder and teasing her nipple through the light, gauzy blouse she wore. "But you do not like public sex, shanna. You have told me this many times."

They passed a couple hard at it on the ground. The woman flung her arms above her head and shouted her approval as a partially clad warrior fucked her at high speed. His pants rested at his knees, and his scabbard slammed the ground with each thrust.

Elise groaned as Ki rubbed her nipple harder. "Maybe I'll make an exception. The spirit of the Festival, and all. Will you join us, Fari?"

The question surprised Fari, and he did not know how to respond. He had been planning to sit with his family, and in point of fact, he was not formally joined with Georgia. No ethic, no law, not even any personal commitment prevented him from finding some relief with his brother's wife. And the way Elise enjoyed double penetration, there would be plenty of relief, if she got into the spirit of the Festival of Seasons.

His cock throbbed, and his body spoke—yet Fari's mind and heart held back. "Thank you," he murmured. "I will sit with you both. Let us see where the afternoon takes us."

That seemed to be enough for Elise. For the rest of their walk, she amused herself by stroking Ki's cock through his tight cloth breeches.

All too soon for Fari's tastes, he was seated beside Elise and Ki in the Royal box.

The Festival enclosure made a giant oval over what had once been Camford's unfettered front lawns. From the Royal box, the Tul'Mars enjoyed an unbroken view of all the bleachers and all the holding boxes. Women from the north, from the south, from east and from the west had been oiled, flowered, and sated enough to maintain basic control during the festivities. Onlookers packed the bleachers, many mated couples—some already fucking hard and fast, in mere anticipation of the action.

Pa marks glittered in the sunslight—every design and pattern imaginable.

On the far end of the now-bleacher-enclosed presenting ground were Arda's stables—and inside the stables, the warriors waited.

Fools, Fari thought. Why couldn't they court and win their mate with more dignity? Did they fear the pitfalls of true "relationship-building," as Elise called it?

Beside him, Ki stirred.

Fari glanced over and saw that his brother had removed his breeches. Elise was stroking his cock with graceful, skilled fingers as she gazed into the excited crowd.

It was then that Fari knew how miserable he would be this afternoon.

What had he been thinking?

He needed to leave this ridiculous display and resume his search for Georgia. Or maybe go to the war room and review what Ki had discovered about Krysta's whereabouts.

A roar rose from the crowd, and Fari turned his attention back to the presentation grounds.

Ten naked warriors, decorated only by *pa*, oils, and loose leather thongs bound about their necks, strode forward.

As they passed each box of maidens, squeals and giggles bubbled and frothed through the warm afternoon air.

The warriors stopped one at a time, spreading their ranks for proper viewing. To a one, their cocks stood erect, showing off some of what they might offer potential mates.

Fari snorted his annoyance.

A handful of naked maidens approached, drawn by physical attraction and initial *psi* compatibility. Three or four each, and for one warrior, almost ten.

The warriors stood passive as the women ran their hands over *pa* marks and pricks alike.

Closest to the Royal box, the first match was made. Four or five women backed away as one woman remained with the stalwart, smiling warrior. She worked his cock with her hand, up and down, while gazing into his eyes.

Fari felt the wave of connection. His own cock stiffened even more, and he cursed.

These were soul's mates. Yes. Any idiot could sense it.

As the woman wrapped a leg around the standing warrior and eased herself onto his waiting erection, Elise groaned. She moved over to Ki, keeping her back to him so she could see the action, and lifted her soft skirts. In one tantalizing move, she sank down on her *sha*'s cock at the same moment the woman and the warrior began to fuck in earnest.

All over the stands, joined couples did likewise.

Fari grabbed his own cock through his breeches and groaned. His mind and heart screamed for Georgia. He wanted to fuck her and only her. Now. *Now!*

You had your chance, you son of a bitch.

Georgia's sharp psi-comment hit Fari so hard he slammed back against his chair — then leaped to his feet.

She was here!

Georgia was at the Festival of Seasons somewhere, but where?

His sharp eyes scanned the crowd one face at a time, but he didn't have to look long.

There. With the southern contingent. Georgia was seated in a maiden's box, stretched out like a queen on a bier. She was oiled, naked, be-flowered, and well-attended. One of the women was toying with her nipples, while another was absently stroking her clit.

Leveling her angry gaze on Fari, Georgia flipped her flaming hair behind her shoulders. Her hips rocked forward, and she spread her legs to give the other maiden better access to her pussy.

Fari gripped the edge of the Royal box so hard the wood splintered.

"Aaah, aaah. Yes. God, yes!" Beside him, Elise bounced on Ki's lap, coming with a burst of shared psi-energy.

As if receiving it, Georgia came, too. She threw her lovely head back and groaned—a sound Fari heard in his mind, felt in his gut.

And suddenly, his shanna's intentions became clear. Georgia had joined the Festival to choose a mate. To deliberately join with another man, thereby ending her relationship with Fari forever.

His brain became a gibbering mash as more warriors filed onto the presentation field.

Georgia gave Fari a wicked grin, then perused the new offerings. Her attention lingered on the soldier closest to her, and she made as if to stand up. As if she might go down to the field and examine Markon. Fari's second in command.

Bellowing, Fari pulled himself forward to vault out of the Royal box.

Damn her.

Revenge.

Elise had warned him.

But he would cross the presentation yard. He would snatch her out of that box, and haul her off for a private discussion.

Strong arms yanked him back.

"No, Brother." Ki's maddeningly cool, sharp voice ripped at Fari's ears. His brother had finished round one with Elise and placed her back in her own seat. Now, he stood behind Fari, restraining him with sure hands. "You have no legal or moral claim on Georgia Steel. She offered herself to you in marriage, and you refused her."

"To Earth's hell with you," Fari growled. He struggled against Ki's iron grasp.

"You broke up with her," Elise added, using the Earth phrase. "She's free to do as she pleases."

Fari stopped short of swearing at Elise. That would certainly be less than honorable.

In the presentation yard, Georgia had indeed climbed down from the box, and she circled Markon with six other prospects.

One of her hands tugged at the leather jesses on his neck, and her other hand found Markon's cock.

Shaking his head like a maddened fergilla bull, Fari exploded back against Ki, driving his brother through the rear boards of the Royal box.

Elise screamed as the brothers fell to the ground one story below. Some of the crowd noticed, but most did not care. Outbursts of rage or passion were not unusual at the Festival of Seasons.

Fari found his feet before Ki, then made use of his one battle advantage over his larger brother.

Speed.

Before Ki could grab him again, Fari turned and ran faster than Arda's surest wind.

Chapter 23

Georgia held on to Markon's prick long enough to be sure Fari had seen her, then gave the big warrior a smile and let him go. Another of the maidens, however, had been captured by the soldier's eyes. A crackle coursed through their *pa*, and Georgia knew the two were meant for each other.

Sighing, she returned to the southern maiden's seats.

When she glanced at the Royal box, she realized Fari was gone.

Figures. Bastard. Coward. Well, he might not have stayed to watch her show, but she *would* find a suitable mate. She'd fuck the guy silly in front of the whole crowd, and somebody would be sure to let Fari know.

Damn him.

Yet even as she sat down, feeling the sensual rub of the soft boards on her naked ass, Georgia knew her heart wasn't in this. One of the maidens reached for her, but Georgia politely declined.

What are you doing? Elise's psi-voice drifted through the chatter Georgia had experienced since she lowered her mental shield.

Moving on, girlfriend. Ooooh, look. New warriors. Georgia forced a light, teasing tone into her thoughts. *Maybe one of these will do.*

Don't, please. Elise sounded desperate.

Look, I love you to death, but stay out of this. Tears competed with Georgia's false cheerfulness. *It's the only way. You know how I am.*

I know how you were, Elise corrected. *A year ago. A world ago. A lifetime ago.*

To keep herself from bursting into sobs, Georgia gently closed off her thoughts again. Elise's honest love and pointed truths were too much. They had always been too much.

Besides, there were rows of fine warriors to explore.

As the suns begin to set on the far western horizon, the next group of warriors made ready to enter the field, and Georgia came close to admitting to herself that she probably couldn't do it—choose, fuck, and marry another man.

Her heart was still set on Fari, and it might be a long bunch of years before she turned loose of wanting that arrogant, temperamental bastard.

One of the priests reached over the box's edge and took her hand. "There is no shame in not finding your mate the first time. It often takes several Festivals."

Georgia forced a smile, but gently extracted her hand.

For some reason, she didn't want to touch anyone. And she didn't want anyone touching her.

In fact, all the fucking was getting on her nerves.

She took a deep breath and closed her eyes. The shield around her thoughts fell away, but she pushed back most of the clatter, chatter, and psi-groaning.

Once more, tears tickled at the corner of Georgia's lids.

If Krysta were here, or even Akad, they would know what to do. Elise would probably help me if I let her. She rubbed the sides of her head. *I suppose I can be as stubborn as Fari. God. I have to stop thinking about him all the time.*

A shocked murmur rippled through the crowd—a new sound. Different enough that Georgia opened her eyes to see what had caused the stir.

The presentation field was nearly empty. Only a few warriors remained, with one standing off from the rest, close to Georgia's box.

Her heart skipped.

No. My mind's playing tricks on me.

But she knew it wasn't.

Fari Tul'Mar stood naked in front of the maiden's box, wearing the leather ties and oils of an available warrior.

Dozens of women flocked toward him, but he ignored them. His gaze remained locked with Georgia as she struggled to believe such an arrogant man could humble himself so completely.

Feeling like she was dreaming, Georgia got up and slowly walked down the wooden bleachers, to the stairs, and out into the field.

More and more women crowded Fari, each eager to possess a Tul'Mar. Georgia could hear their thoughts. About his muscles. His handsome face. The black depths of his eyes. The blaze of his *pa*. His magnificent cock.

They were touching him everywhere, but Fari didn't so much as twitch.

"Excuse me." Georgia snatched the first woman and shoved her aside. The next woman thought about resisting, but Georgia's laser-glare must have persuaded her otherwise.

"No. Not! Bitch. Get your hands off him." With a few well-placed bumps, nudges, snatches, and outright kicks, Georgia cleared most of her path to Fari.

The crowd rumbled and roared, eager to see what would come of this showdown. Georgia was vaguely aware of Elise's nervous thoughts and Ki's subtle encouragements.

To Fari? To her?

Georgia couldn't tell.

She reached Fari and parted the last wave of admiring women with a single, sharp psi-command.

Back the fuck off.

It might have been Earth slang, but the meaning was clear enough.

Reluctantly, though with respect for Georgia's heightened psi-powers, the women excused themselves and made way for Georgia's approach.

In moments, Georgia stood alone with Fari, the last couple left on the presentation field. She was close enough to kick him, but she slapped him instead.

The crowd murmured.

Fari didn't blink, and he still didn't move.

Georgia slapped him again. God, but that felt good.

And yet he kept his intense, brooding eyes fastened on her like a determined tiger, gazing at prey.

"You're a bastard," she said. "Did you know that?"

"Yes." Fari's tone was even. And soft again. His cock wasn't soft, though. It stood rigid and ready, and his breathing came in short gasps.

Georgia could literally feel how much he wanted her. His desire made her *pa* sizzle.

Damn him!

She grabbed the thongs of Fari's leather collar and jerked him forward.

He didn't resist.

"I ought to kick you right in the nuts." In a fit of pique, she shoved him back a step, and Fari sank to one knee, still looking at her with those electric black eyes.

"Why are you doing this?" Georgia demanded.

"Because I am deeply sorry for being a bastard. And for hurting you."

Georgia kicked at the dirt beside him. "Not good enough."

"I know." Fari at last broke their stare and lowered his head. "But if you see fit to give me time and another chance, I will make it good enough."

Georgia hesitated.

She had an urge to choke the jerk with his leather collar. And she knew he might not even try to stop her.

Instead, she dropped the jesses. "Get up. I'm not interested. Let's just end this here and now, so both of us can move on."

Fari stood. The lines of his face were hard, but not angry. More hurt.

Georgia's heart clenched.

"We are alike, you and I. Both running from old pains, living with old wounds." Fari reached one hand forward and cupped her cheek. Georgia tried to pull away, but he wouldn't let her. "I was wrong not to tell you of mine, and to let my past come between us. With your help, I can heal those old scars. Perhaps we might heal together."

"Go to hell," she whispered, but she didn't mean it.

Fari cupped her other cheek and drew her forward, until their lips met in a soft, lingering kiss.

Georgia was aware of cheering, but it sounded faint and distant as Fari pulled back.

"One more chance," he whispered. His black eyes were wide and sincere. "I will not let you down a second time."

"And if I say yes?" Georgia moved against him, feeling the thrill of his hard body against hers, enjoying his stiff cock pressed into her belly. Her *pa* tingled with his, and bit by bit, their thoughts reconnected.

If you say yes, I will fuck you here and now. I will bring you to orgasm for all to see, and you will be my wife, my soul's mate, forever.

Air left Georgia's lungs in a rush. She closed her eyes as Fari eased his hands down her shoulders to her breasts and pinched her nipples.

His fingers felt like hot pincers, setting her skin on fire.

"No more doubts?" she muttered, grabbing his collar's thongs and pressing her breasts into his grip.

"None." He bent down and captured one pebbled nipple in his teeth. *Look around you*, shanna. *All of these people can see your pleasure. Will you still deny me?*

193

Georgia did glance around the stands.

Thousands of eyes watched as Fari suckled one nipple, then the other. Her pussy felt like a chamber of fire, screaming for entry.

Fari turned her around and held her against him, still fondling her breasts. His cock pressed into her ass, and still, Georgia kept hold of his jesses.

This was too hot for words.

Here and there, couples started to fuck—Elise and Ki among them. The erotic charge in the air was so intense Georgia didn't know if she could stand it.

You can stand this, Fari assured her. *And more. Infinitely more.*

He eased his hands down to her hips, then bent her forward slightly. Georgia pulled on the long collar thongs to keep her balance—and to keep Fari close to her.

He nudged her legs apart with the damp tip of his cock, and she spread them wide. He pulled back against the jesses with his strong neck, helping her keep her balance.

And still, he teased her, easing just the tip of his hard staff into her waiting juices.

Georgia moved her hips from side to side, watching all the people watching her. "Put it in me," she said, surprised by the rasp in her voice. "You always make me wait."

"You have no room to talk on that account," Fari murmured. He slipped his cock in another fraction, then pulled back out.

Georgia's nipples ached as her breasts bounced from the contact. She groaned with frustration.

In the stands, women and men yelled and screamed with orgasms. The smell of sex hung heavy in the twilight air.

Georgia jerked the collar thongs and leaned back into Fari's cock. "Fuck me, you arrogant bastard. I'm not asking again."

With a growl of pleasure, Fari grabbed her hips, bent her over further, and rammed his rigid staff into Georgia's waiting slit.

She pulled hard on the jesses to keep from falling, but Fari's firm grip on her hips steadied her.

"Keep your eyes open, shanna. See everything you can." He pumped in and out of her as she moaned with the sweet feel of his length in her pussy. "This is your last fuck as an unmarried woman. When you come, you are mine for all times."

"And...you're...mine!" Georgia bit her lip, lost in the feel of his hammering cock. God, but he filled her up. Ramming higher. Deeper.

Hundreds of minds filled with the sounds and sensations of her pleasure, and she enjoyed making each of them hornier than hell.

Heat consumed her pussy, spilling out to her belly, and upward, taking her like a slow-burning fire.

Fari fucked her harder, and only the jesses and his tightening grip around her waist kept her on her feet. Each thrust lifted her from the ground and made her cry out with satisfaction.

Fari freed a hand and caught one of her nipples and pinched it. He jerked her against him, still plunging into her like a man deprived for years. She felt his hot breath on her neck as she straightened up.

"Now," Fari whispered, lowering her until his fingers slipped into her wet curls. "Keep those eyes open. Do not forget this. Never forget this."

His finger found her clit in seconds, and then he possessed her totally. Filling her pussy. Pinching her nipple. Stroking her clit. Biting her neck. Holding her up as he did it, for everyone to look. For everyone to see how he fucked her.

Georgia felt like a limp doll, helpless against the intense pleasure. Her pussy walls squeezed against his cock, and they both shouted and came at the same time—along with half of the onlookers.

"Georgia!" Ki bellowed from the stands, loud enough to be heard a planet away. "Shanna Fari Tul'Mar! Shanna Fari Tul'Mar!"

"Yes!" Fari shouted.

"Yes!" Georgia echoed.

The crowd let loose with another ear-splitting set of cheers.

Elise was clapping and shouting too.

You did it, she told Georgia proudly through her psi-link. *I'm so happy for you!*

Fari's slipped his cock from Georgia's pussy, picked her up, and began to carry her from the presentation field. Where they were headed, Georgia had no idea—but she hoped it was back to Ammon Island.

At least for a few days. Or maybe a few years.

In the back of her sex-sated brain, she let herself fully realize what had just happened—and she welcomed the knowledge with her whole heart and being.

Georgia Steel, formerly of Earth and now forever of Arda, had just become the Sailkeeper's bride.

Epilogue

Chuck Sampson positioned the hidden video camera behind his bedroom armchair.

"They never look there," he said, smug in his certainty that all women were fundamentally stupid—at least when they wanted to fuck.

In ten minutes, the lovely Tina would arrive. A twenty-year-old student from his advanced theory of law class. She needed help on her grade—after a few key harsh grades from Chuck, of course—and he had offered a little private tutoring.

The wide-eyed young woman agreed without questions.

She wanted it. She had to want it. Only a naïve bimbo would come to a professor's house late at night and expect to go home with her chastity intact.

"No fuck, no pass. Yep. Best class policy I ever made." Chuck straightened his smoking jacket, smoothed his silk pants, and ran his hands through his blond hair. It was still thick.

He hadn't lost a thing since high school.

Women loved him.

Some men thought they were God's gift to the female sex—but Chuck knew the truth. He *was* God's gift.

The doorbell rang.

Chuck nearly ran to answer it, then made himself slow to a respectable stroll.

Tina stood on his stoop, shivering even though it was fairly warm outside.

"Come in, come in." Chuck gave her his most winning smile. God, she was hot. Red hair, big boobs, an ass to die for—not unlike Georgia Steel. One of his first conquests. Chuck hadn't thought about her in years, but his dick got hard at just the memory.

She'd put up a big fight, yelling *no*, scratching and clawing—but they all did, until he got 'em down and gave 'em what they needed. Yep. Georgia Steel had been one hot piece of ass.

Just like Tina would be.

The girl sat down in a leather chair in Chuck's living room, clutching her books in front of her. "Thanks for agreeing to help me, Professor. I don't know what could have happened on those exams. I studied so hard."

Chuck's erection strained his pants.

Should he dispense with seduction and fuck her right now? That tight sweater. The short skirt. She sure as hell deserved a good poking.

No. No. Take you time. This is sweet. Savor it.

"My pleasure," Chuck said affably. "Now. Why don't you come on over here to the couch, and we'll get started."

Tina stood, still trembling, and eased over to join him—just as a rustle from the back of the house caught Chuck's attention.

Damn. Did the camera fall?

"Do you have a dog?" Tina's wide-eyed expression just wouldn't quit.

"Uh, no. Let me go check that out." Chuck stood. "On second thought, why don't you come with me? I'll show you the house."

Yeah. That's the ticket. The old here's the den, here's the kitchen, here's the bedroom and the bii-iig, lonely bed. That gets 'em every time.

Hesitating but compliant, Tina nodded and followed after him as he led her through the maze of rooms toward his ultimate destination—the big lonely bed where he planned to fuck her silly.

The tour went well. Chuck took his time pointing out rooms, books, statues, paintings—all the while managing to stand closer and closer to little Tina. She still had her books, but he'd get rid of those soon enough.

"And this," he said with a flourish, at last reaching target: bedroom, "is where I do my best work."

Tina straightened beside him and tried to inch away, back around him and out of the room.

"Hey, hey, there." Chuck grabbed her by both arms. She dropped her books. "Don't run away so fast. Don't you want to get a feel for my biii-iig, lonely bed? It could really use some company."

"You bastard." Tina struggled against his grip. "I don't want to sleep with you! I came here to study. You said you'd help me!"

"And I will. No fuck, no pass. Simple as that." Chuck grinned. It was all downhill from here.

"God. You men are all the same!" Tina tried to kick him, but missed.

"I beg to differ," said an incredibly low bass voice from the shadows behind the bedroom recliner.

A man stepped out into the open, and Chuck felt his dick shrivel up.

This guy was big. No. Huge. He was wearing pirate clothes—a loose-laced tunic and breeches, and for God's sake, there was a freaky-looking sword in a scabbard, hanging against his tree-trunk leg.

"I—I—have a security system," Chuck managed to squeak.

The big man ignored him. He strode forward and grabbed Chuck by the shoulder, peeling him away from Tina like he was nothing more than a half-dead leech.

Chuck dove for the phone, trying to grab the handset to dial 9-1-1.

Effortlessly, the giant snatched the base and handset, threw it to the floor, and crushed it with one stomp. To Tina, he said in heavily accented but proper English, "All men are not the same. In fact, most bear no resemblance to this worthless piece of *fergilla* dung. Find yourself a better specimen. You certainly deserve more."

"Who are you?" Tina whispered as the big man knelt and picked up her books. She gaped at the silvery marks visible through his tunic's loose laces. "And what is that tattoo on your chest?"

"I am a friend." The man smiled. He handed Tina her books. "Now go, and leave this low-life bastard to me."

Chuck couldn't believe his ears. "Tina! Don't do it! Run. Get out of here and call the police!"

Tina hesitated for only a moment. Then, with a satisfied smile, she turned to Chuck. "Go fuck yourself."

To the strange giant, she said, "Thanks. He's all yours. Though I can't imagine why anybody would want *him*."

The giant winked. "The universe is a vast place, little one. Even Chuck of Earth may be of use to some."

High above Earth, in shielded orbit on the *pa*-coated decks of *Lorelei*, Georgia Steel waited. She wasn't nervous. She wasn't even angry.

Just...eager. Almost too eager.

She fingered the soft fabric of Fari's tunic, belted around her waist like a short dress. Her ruby blades hung from that belt, and she felt the soft fergilla-hide scabbards against her bare legs. On her feet, she wore a pair of Ardani flat sandals, thick enough to protect her feet, but thin enough to feel the thrum of *Lorelei*'s engines and the hum of the ship's *pa* coating.

Ah. The little pleasures of her new life.

The speeder was coming. She could see it. As she smiled, her heart rate increased.

Fari, she projected.

His response was immediate. *Beloved.*

You're late.

I apologize. I had some technological items to destroy—"tapes" I believe they are called. And a young woman needed safe return to her dormitory.

Bastard. He hasn't changed a bit, has he?

Fari's psi-chuckle gave Georgia delicious body-chills. *He is balding on top, his belly is larger than it should be—and this stain on the front of his pants—most unbecoming.*

At this, Georgia burst into outright laughter. The skeleton crew glanced up from their various positions, but none of them stared. They were used to Georgia by now. She was the first Fleet spouse ever to insist on accompanying her *sha* on military missions, and she rarely left Fari's side.

This, however, was no military mission. Not really. It was more diplomatic, and thus the newly reconstituted Galactic Council had approved it without much argument.

Georgia watched the speeder draw closer, extend docking clamps, and pull alongside *Lorelei*.

Just knowing Fari was closer made her pussy wet. They had been married for close to one stellar month, and she stayed well-fucked and fully satisfied all the time. The joy was so deep and sweet, so total. If only they could find Krysta and Akad, her happiness would be complete.

But soon enough for that. Ki had intelligence scouts all over the galaxy, and they had returned some basic information about the location of Outlander bases.

That was a fight for another day—a day coming very soon.

As for now, Georgia and the Sailkeeper were cleaning up some simpler unfinished business.

Taking out a little galactic trash, Georgia thought.

The speeder finished docking, and *Lorelei's* inertial dampeners enveloped the returned pod like a welcome child.

The hatch popped open.

Fari stepped out and psi-called to two of the crew. *Bind up this ass, and bring him out.*

The warriors hurried over and entered the speeder, leaving Fari free to stride over, grab Georgia, spin her around, and give her a deep kiss.

Even hours apart feel too long, shanna.

Georgia hung on his neck. *I love you so much. You know that right?*

Without question. Fari nudged her belly with his erection. *After we empty this "trash," as you termed him, I'll expect a little proof of that sentiment.*

"Want it now?" Georgia grinned and squeezed his hard cock through his breeches.

"Hey!" came a high-pitched squeal from behind them. It barely sounded human, much less male. Thumps and curses told Georgia the warriors had hauled Chuck onto *Lorelei's* decks and thrown him down in total disgust.

Georgia let go of Fari and felt her lips curl into a half-smile, half-snarl. She winked at her husband. "Bring him to me, will you?"

Fari bowed and beckoned to his warriors.

Georgia heard a loud thud.

She turned around, and for the first time in years, her gaze fell on Chuck Sampson.

On his knees. With his hands tied behind his back. He was dressed in some ridiculous red robe-jacket and silk pants—wet and stinking from when he pissed on himself, probably more than once. Fari was right. The top of Chuck's head was going bald.

She expected to feel something—fear, anger, sadness—but her only emotion was amusement, and a distant sort of satisfaction. A feeling of rightness, like the universe coming full circle.

"Well, well, well. How's it hanging, buddy?" Georgia kicked Chuck in the shoulder. Not hard enough to knock him over. Just enough to get his attention. "Or is it too limp to hang these days? Guess it just lays there like an old rotten noodle, unless you can find a girl to rape. That's the only thing that gets you off, right?"

"Georgia?" Chuck straightened up and spread his knees wider for balance. He slowly raised his eyes. "Georgia Steel?"

Fari smacked the back of his head. "Georgia Tul'Mar. Speak her name wrong again, and die."

"That silver stuff's all over you." Chuck whimpered, and the stain on his pants widened. "This has to be a dream. It can't be real."

Georgia laughed, then crooked her finger and slid it under Chuck's chin. "Oh it's real. Believe it now or later, your choice. But I'd suggest now. You'll need all your wits and then some in about an hour. Oh. What am I saying? You have no wits. Just like you have no dick."

Fari snickered.

The *Lorelei* started to move. It was a subtle feeling, but Georgia knew the ship had already jumped to light speed. They were streaking past Jupiter, Saturn—and faster, the planets blurred as they left the Terran system.

Chuck whined a little more, struggled with his bonds, then finally formed a few coherent words. "What do you want with me?"

Georgia drew her swords with lightning speed and slammed both ruby blades between Chuck's legs. Through fabric. Mere threads away from either side of his pathetic penis. "*I* wanted to cut your dick off, take you back to Arda, and let my husband and his brother teach you some respect for women."

"Ah-ah-ah," Chuck stammered, staring at the swords. His shoulders quivered as he pulled on the ropes that tied his hands, and he sounded like an engine running out of gas.

It made Georgia happy to watch him sweat. She beckoned for Fari, who joined her in front of Chuck's now-frozen form. She put her arms around her husband's neck and kissed him, letting one hand travel down to give his hard cock an affectionate squeeze.

"This, Chuckie," she murmured, "is a real man. With a real cock. And real brains, too. Alien concepts for you, I know."

Keeping her arms around Fari, Georgia gave Chuck one more disdainful glance. "Like I said, I wanted to cut your dick off, but my husband had a better idea. We're taking you to a place where men like you belong."

"H-Hell?" Chuck stammered, still petrified into stony stillness by the sharp red blades nearly biting into his dick.

Fari laughed.

So did Georgia.

Without a second thought, she turned her back on the bastard and walked away, intent on fucking her husband before they reached the rendezvous point. Quickies were a blast, especially in the observation nest, at top stellar speeds.

Fari felt immense satisfaction as *Lorelei* slowed to allow the huge purple ship to dock less than one Earth hour later. He helped Georgia down from the observation nest, and the two of them were surprised to find Chuck still pinned by Georgia's swords.

"Guess the warriors don't have any respect or compassion for pathetic, whimpering rapists," Georgia noted.

Fari glanced at the few members of his crew brave enough to remain above deck and greet their frightening visitors. They looked like thunderheads, to a one, and their thoughts were of murder and torture.

"No respect at all, shanna."

An eerie, keening wail filled the vast silence of space, and Fari shivered in spite of himself.

A stampede of bare feet let him know that Chuck's new friends had arrived.

Though he wasn't likely to see it that way.

"Get your swords, beloved." He gave Georgia's ass a pinch. "And cut him loose. They'll be in a hurry."

Georgia nodded. She squared off with Chuck once more and retrieved her ruby blades, cut Chuck's bonds with a single hack, then sheathed the swords with deft, graceful skill.

"What's happening?" Chuck demanded as he struggled to his feet.

"Your escort is here." Georgia gestured over Chuck's shoulder. "They've come to take you to your new home."

"You're not going to—to kill me?" Foolish Chuck actually sounded relieved. He didn't turn around. Another foolish move, in Fari's estimation.

"Wouldn't dream of it." Georgia smiled. "I'm better than you in that respect. Well, in all respects. So, no. I won't kill you. Let's call this protective custody, for the good of all the women back on Earth. Meet your new friends, Chuck. They'll be really glad to get to know God's gift to the female species."

And then Chuck did turn around.

Fari thought the pathetic bastard might have screamed, but who could hear such a little noise over the chaos of Bandu mating calls.

Twenty towering wild women descended on Chuck, sweeping him away in one great, thrashing purple wave.

The flash of chains, ankle bracelets, and wristcuffs threw light across the deck, and many of the Ardani warriors turned their heads away.

Chuck of Earth would be lucky if the crazed female warriors didn't fuck him to death before they got him home.

Then again, it might be better for the bastard if they did.

Life on Bandu-Mother was difficult for men, to say the least. Especially weak men. Ah, well. Chuck was about to understand existence as a second-class citizen, judged solely on the basis of his gender.

"Hope he has fun," Georgia said, waving happily as the last of the Bandu boarded ship.

In minutes, the purple craft pulled away.

Fari captured his shanna by the waist, pulling her against him and into a gentle hug. "It was my great pleasure to arrange this for you, beloved. One door of pain, forever closed. Chuck will never hurt another Earth female."

"Mmm. I know." Georgia reached back and grabbed Fari's hips, rubbing herself against his cock. "I think I owe you a few rounds of thanks, yes?"

"No. But I will accept payment."

"How many times can we fuck before Lorelei makes it back to Arda? Ten? Maybe fifteen?"

"I do not know." Fari stepped back, took Georgia's hand, and started to lead her toward the Captain's cabin.

"No. Not there." Georgia's voice sounded husky and aroused.

Fari stopped, turned around, and gathered Georgia to him again. He kissed his shanna hard on the mouth.

She slipped her hand into his breeches and grabbed his cock. Moving against her sweet grip, Fari asked, *Where, then, beloved?*

Georgia's psi-laugh warmed him through and through. *I'm kind of partial to that observation nest. What do you say?*

I say…first one to the top chooses positions. He let her go and dashed for the rigging.

"Last one up gets to come first!" Georgia shouted, running hard behind him.

Fari climbed as fast as he could, certain she would cut the ropes from beneath his hands if she gained any ground.

Of course she would.

My warrior. My Lorelei. Shanna. I love you now and always.

Sha, came Georgia's loving response, even as her ruby blades slashed at the rigging he was climbing. *I love you, too. But if you think that'll save your sorry ass, you've got another think coming…*

The Arda Collection

Glossary

Akad	High Priest of Arda, marked with *pa* like henna tattoos on his cheeks.
Ammon Island	Private tropical getaway on Arda, owned by Fari Tul'Mar.
Arda	40,000 stellar years old. Home planet of Ki, Fari, Krysta, and the Royal Fleet. It is famous for its metallurgy, fine castles, magnificent Chimera, and towering warriors. Arthurian in rule and structure, but enlightened and modern, Arda has an excellent reputation in the Free Galaxy. Ardani citizens carry *pa*-marks, and most are psychic. The generous and respected Tul'Mar clan has ruled them for thousands of years.
Astoria	Flagship in Arda's Royal Fleet.
Bandu	Fierce purple fighting women, valued by OrTan slavers.

Camford	Palatial ancestral home of the Tul'Mar clan.
Camford Forest	Thick woods surrounding Camford's grounds.
Chimera	Multicolored horse-like creatures native to Arda, with giraffe and unicorn features.
Coscans	Blue aliens often enslaved by the OrTans; females have a single breast.
Darkyn Weil	Mysterious leader of the Outlanders. Age, unknown. Birth place or circumstance, also unknown. He carries a double-headed axe with yellow blades that match his yellow eyes.
Denovan	Furry, manlike, very stinky aliens. Often make use of OrTan pleasure slaves.
Elise Ashton	28 Earth years old, blond hair, blue eyes. Dreams of a spacepirate rescuing her from her boring life.
Fari Tul'Mar	Sailkeeper of Arda. Brother to Ki and Krysta, guardian of the Sailmaster and the Royal Fleet. 120 stellar years old, marked with *pa* in the shape of a great winged bird on his chest. He carries a barbed, spiked sapphire blade.

Fergilla beasts	Ugly, hairy white buffalo-like beasts native to Arda, often used in name-calling and insults.
Festival of Seasons	Ardani celebration of the harvest. Involves mating of unwed citizens.
Galactic Council	Ruling body of the known and free planets. Mediates disputes, but has some vulnerability to treachery and bribery.
Gasha	OrTan pleasure bed.
Georgia Steel	28 Earth years old, auburn hair, green eyes. Distant cousin of Elise Ashston's, raised as her sister.
Ki Tul'Mar	Sailmaster of Arda. Brother to Fari and Krysta. 150 stellar years old, marked with *pa* in a flame pattern beginning at his waist, dividing on his chest, and flaming up both shoulders. He carries a diamond blade that matches his shanna's eyes.
Kon'pa	Ardani Dance of Life, to honor *pa*, the stars, and the sails of the Royal Fleet.
Krysta Tul'Mar	Captain of the Ardani Home Guard. Sister to Ki and Fari. 100 stellar years old, marked with *pa* in a soft pattern like cherry blossoms on her chest and neck.

Law of Keeping	Ardani law governing the claiming of a Sailmaster's mate.
Lord Gith	OrTan prince and slaver.
Lorelei	Three mythical guardians of the Tul'Mar line, halflings, often depicted as feral with cat-like features.
Ma'ord'pa	The end of life; the end of time. The doom of Ardani civilization.
Nostans	Tiny species, approximately three feet in height, who frequent OrTan pleasure ships.
Ord'pa	Ceremonial Ardani executioner.
OrTa	Planet in the Free Galaxy still engaged in the forbidden and heavily policed practice of pleasure slaving. OrTans are large and humanoid, but scaled.
OrTan collar	Collar used on pleasure slaves to ensure compliance through pain. Also translates multiple languages for the wearer.
OrTan pain stick	Long staff with electrical tip used for subduing OrTan pleasure slaves.
Outlanders	A faction of Ardani citizens thought to be without *pa* marks or psi-powers. They live reclusively and study old wisdom to prevent the "end of time," which they believe to be coming soon.

Pa	The living substance that created and makes up the life force of the universe.
Royal Fleet	Ardani space frigates, sloops, and speeders commanded by Ki Tul'Mar.
Sha	Ardani soul's mate (male).
Shanna	Ardani soul's mate (female).
Skull	OrTan combat or pleasure ship (slaving vessel), shaped like a humanoid skull.
Tanna Kon'pa	"The People"; what the Outlanders call themselves.
Tuscan Platform	Ancient site of Ardani rituals, located in the center of the Camford Forest.

Enjoy this excerpt from
Arda: The Captain's Fancy
© Copyright Annie Windsor 2004

All Rights Reserved, Ellora's Cave Publishing, Inc.

"I cannot kill *Barung*." Arda's *Ord'pa*, the most fearsome and renowned executioner in the civilized worlds, shook his head. The black of his unfettered hair seemed deep and endless in contrast to the startling silver stripes on his taut cheeks. "He is too powerful. The energy he stored during his rising would disperse and destroy us all. Perhaps the known universe with us."

The expression he wore, of burden and seriousness beyond measure, was shared by Kaldor, First Priest of Kaerad, the eldest among the three. Kaldor sat at the Tower's round table, a table Earth's kings of men would one day hold dear. He used the circular structure to keep a healthy physical distance from his two fellow Council members. Kaeradi were empaths of the first order, telempaths, in fact. Not only could flesh-contact with an incompatible bring great pain or even death to the Kaeradi, but the projection of that pain could kill the innocent who touched them as well.

Kaldor had a physical look similar to the *Ord'pa*, to the Ardani in general, but without the universe's living substance etched into his flesh. He had instead a great golden stone set into his chest just above his heart. Gold was the color of a spiritually transformed leader, of a mystic who had achieved the highest disciplines. Gold was for the fire that lived in stone, and it was this gold flesh-rock he touched in a gesture of weary defeat.

"So." He sighed, sitting back. "We have contained the evil by a combination of our strengths, but we cannot destroy it."

"I refuse to accept that." Myrddin of Perth, and now of Earth only since Perth was no more, stood and went to gaze out of the tower windows. Avalon stretched before him, bright, sparkling, and new. All that was good in this world frolicked on the verdant fields, both those with deep magik and those with the younger, wilder variety bred of this planet alone. Perthling, Ardani, Kaeradi, or halfling mingled with the lesser-developed humans of this world — it mattered not. All were welcome. All were joyous and free to be what the universe called them to be. Earth had fulfilled its promise thus far, as a haven for those fleeing the darkest necromancer ever to rise to power in the universe.

Barung. Lord of the Dark. Eater of Light. Scourge of Souls.

Such dramatic names.

Myrddin sighed.

Even now, he could feel the bastard's malevolence radiating from the containment field established above Earth. The true horror came in how quickly people could forget such amorality. In a few generations, the children of Avalon would have no memory of evil as great as *Barung.* They scarcely understood now, even one generation removed from the devastation wrought on Kaerad, Arda, and his own destroyed world of Perth. Their blood would be mingled, and the unique gifts of each race lost — or melded to create something even more wondrous. Such things were not to be known until they happened.

Well, the Kaeradi priest probably knew, at least in the sketchy non-descript colors of future emotion he could see, but he was wise enough not to share his vague predictive visions.

"I know your grief is deep, Brother Myrddin," the *Ord'pa* of Arda allowed. His accent made the name sound more like "Mertin" or "Merlyn," which was how many of

Avalon's children hailed him already. "The loss of Perth was tragic, and the ripples will be felt in the fabric of time until the last breath on the last world at the last moment of time. Alas, despite the rightness of our vengeance, even I do not have the power to kill *Barung*. If we blended all of our great skills together, we would still be doomed to failure."

For a time, silence claimed the round table in the round room, in the round tower on the round hill.

Circles, Myrddin thought. *Powerful and yet powerless.*

Kaldor cleared his throat. "We could...banish him, could we not? Bind him in his own squalid energy and send him into other dimensions to find his way back—if he can?"

"And visit his evil on some other peoples? Leave him to return and destroy our children eons hence?" Myrddin snorted even as he saw a dawning agreement on the solemn face of the *Ord'pa*. Perthling blood ran hotter than Ardani blood, without doubt. Arda was about balance—this with that, strength with restraint. Perthling blood ran hotter still than the blood of the Kaeradi, who had more power than any, and an even greater reticence to use it. Perth's greatest wizard wanted death for his people's vengeance. More than that, Myrddin wanted a permanent end to the threat.

"Come, Myrddin." Kaldor's tone took a definitive depth, an absolute command only a Kaeradi could achieve without offending any listeners. "Acknowledge this as our only choice. You cannot deny the truths before us."

"I will not doom the worlds of tomorrow to the fate Perth suffered." Myrddin turned and rapped his fist on the round table. A sound like thunder burst through the room as wild magik skittered over wood, then stones.

Instinctively, the Kaeradi priest and the *Ord'pa* flung up their hands and concentrated their energies on blocking Myrddin's rage-spell before it did harm.

The Tor's tower trembled as the magiks met and intertwined. A few of the stones exploded, leaving menacing, crackling black holes where they once stood. The air took on a sudden smell of burning and melting, and a light smoke curled above the round table in the unmistakable shape of a feather.

Kaldor watched the display without passion, but the *Ord'pa* narrowed his eyes at the smoke-feather, at the flashing streaks of magikal light, in truth, a brief harnessing of the living substance of the universe. Myrddin knew the Ardani was thinking. He could almost hear the man's scientific mind observing, planning. Perhaps "plotting" would be a better word?

Myrddin narrowed his own eyes, studying the executioner. The Ardani *were* a crafty lot. Great thinkers and innovators, much as Perthlings had developed a reputation as naturalists and healers. Kaeradi were deep into emotion, the spiritual arts and the rhythm of the universe. All three races bred virulent warriors, though their weapons were decidedly different. Arda fought with science and the focused energy of the mind, Kaerad with the fire of the heart and resolve of the spirit, and Perth with the force of the body and natural elements.

"What are you contemplating?" Myrddin asked quietly, in deference to the *Ord'pa*'s renewed alertness.

The Ardani clenched his hands before him in the gesture of a supplicant. "Our joined powers cannot defeat

Barung...now." The silver stripes on his cheeks glittered with sudden manic energy. "We would have to banish the blackheart, yes. For now. But with forethought and cooperation, we could deliberately crossbreed our races and mingle them with the wild energies of this world to build the strength we need. We could also use Perth's destruction to good ends, laying the proper traps in the energy signature of the universe where the planet once orbited..."

"That would take thousands of years," Myrddin said carefully, measuring each word so that Kaldor and the *Ord'pa* might heed him instead of humoring him. "Time carves memory like sand carves stone. How can we be certain tomorrow's children will know that we existed, much less that we planned for a disaster we doomed them to endure?"

"Nothing is ever certain, Myrddin." Kaldor's calm galled Myrddin, but he kept his mouth clamped as the old Kaeradi spoke. "Better we leave our children many healthy years — and some hope — rather than none, yes?"

For that question, Myrddin, despite his powerful passions to the contrary, had no good answer. He closed his eyes.

When he opened them a few seconds later, the *Ord'pa* was busy drawing pictures, his long graceful fingers borrowing liquid energy from his silver tattoos to create wispy designs on the round table and in the air. A triangle, with three planets — Earth, Kaerad, and Arda — at the corners. In the center, the Ardani sketched a dark hole where Perth should have been, and showed how, with a few alterations in solar winds and the pressures and energies of space, an unsuspecting ship or even an entire world might be sucked into that void and crushed into nothingness. Much the way *Barung* crushed Perth, in fact. With the weight of the universe itself, turned on a single point.

Myrddin watched in silent surrender as Kaldor invested in this far-future design, and began to speak of setting celestial events into play that would produce such a world-crushing void.

Then the talk turned to creating and nurturing bloodlines, and how to establish and maintain channels of energy between the three planets that could one day ensnare Barung in Perth's dead space like a fly in an Earth spider's web.

This is fantasy, Myrddin told himself, but as he studied the plan and listened to the *Ord'pa*'s hypnotic bass, a small hope caught fire in his heart. He thought about the relative nature of triumph over an evil as great as *Barung*.

In truth, *Barung* was more creature than person. *Barung* created himself from his own evil intent, from the dark energy he drew from the very pit of the universe. It overwhelmed him, turned him into naught but a twisted, deformed channel, absorbing every negative thought in his purview, every wicked action. Violence, hate, cruelty — *Barung* became a living embodiment of all such bleakness. The Council had joined to bind him with their combined magiks.

With our different commands of the energies of the universe, Myrddin corrected himself automatically, as the *Ord'pa* would have if the wizard had spoken aloud. *Know and name the power you wield, lest your children forget it.*

Myrddin flexed his arms, wishing he could wield those powers to dispel the non-corporeal Barung himself.

But he knew he could not. The Kaeradi priest and the Ardani executioner were correct. Destroying the necromancer would release every drop of that formless blackness *Barung* had absorbed, and the wave of dark energy would sweep the universe of hope and joy, light and life.

Unless they could trick the beast into the void.

And the void wasn't created yet, nor the powers that might drive the beast to it without chance of escape.

Banishment was the only option.

But one day, Myrddin thought with increasing vengeance, *Barung will return.* He stared at the shimmering triangle as it turned from silver to gold in the waning daylight. The triangle with the dark center, even now flickering above and across the round table of Earth's tower on the Tor. *If the universe is willing, the Council will rise again then, stronger than ever.*

His mind turned to the writing of scrolls and books and sacred teachings, to the leaving of monuments in stone and iron and every conceivable medium—one hundred ways to pass the needed knowledge through the ages, in case something should happen to him.

It was later that same night, still at the round table in the round tower on the round hill, that he penned the one scroll that the old Kaeradi could have told him would indeed survive, worlds away from its writing.

About the author:

Annie Windsor is 37 years old and lives in Tennessee with her two children and nine pets (as of today's count). Annie's a southern girl, though like most magnolias, she has steel around that soft heart. Does she have a drawl? Of course, though she'll deny it, y'all. She dreams of being a full-time writer, and looks forward to the day she can spend more time on her mountain farm. She loves animals, sunshine, and good fantasy novels. On a perfect day, she writes, reads, spends time with her family, chats with friends, and discovers nothing torn, eaten, or trampled by her beloved puppies or crafty kitties.

Annie welcomes mail from readers. You can write to her c/o Ellora's Cave Publishing at 1337 Commerce Drive, Suite 13, Stow OH 44224.

Why an electronic book?

We live in the Information Age—an exciting time in the history of human civilization in which technology rules supreme and continues to progress in leaps and bounds every minute of every hour of every day. For a multitude of reasons, more and more avid literary fans are opting to purchase e-books instead of paperbacks. The question to those not yet initiated to the world of electronic reading is simply: *why?*

1. *Price.* An electronic title at Ellora's Cave Publishing runs anywhere from 40-75% less than the cover price of the <u>exact same title</u> in paperback format. Why? Cold mathematics. It is less expensive to publish an e-book than it is to publish a paperback, so the savings are passed along to the consumer.

2. *Space.* Running out of room to house your paperback books? That is one worry you will never have with electronic novels. For a low one-time cost, you can purchase a handheld computer designed specifically for e-reading purposes. Many e-readers are larger than the average handheld, giving you plenty of screen room. Better yet, hundreds of titles can be stored within your new library—a single microchip. (Please note that Ellora's Cave does not endorse any specific brands. You can check our website at www.ellorascave.com for customer recommendations we make available to new consumers.)

3. *Mobility.* Because your new library now consists of only a microchip, your entire cache of books can be taken with you wherever you go.

4. *Personal preferences are accounted for.* Are the words you are currently reading too small? Too large? Too...**ANNOYING**? Paperback books cannot be modified according to personal preferences, but e-books can.

5. *Innovation.* The way you read a book is not the only advancement the Information Age has gifted the literary community with. There is also the factor of what you can read. Ellora's Cave Publishing will be introducing a new line of interactive titles that are available in e-book format only.

6. *Instant gratification.* Is it the middle of the night and all the bookstores are closed? Are you tired of waiting days—sometimes weeks—for online and offline bookstores to ship the novels you bought? Ellora's Cave Publishing sells instantaneous downloads 24 hours a day, 7 days a week, 365 days a year. Our e-book delivery system is 100% automated, meaning your order is filled as soon as you pay for it.

Those are a few of the top reasons why electronic novels are displacing paperbacks for many an avid reader. As always, Ellora's Cave Publishing welcomes your questions and comments. We invite you to email us at service@ellorascave.com or write to us directly at: 1337 Commerce Drive, Suite 13, Stow OH 44224.

Discover for yourself why readers can't get enough of the multiple award-winning publisher Ellora's Cave. Whether you prefer e-books or paperbacks, be sure to visit EC on the web at www.ellorascave.com for an erotic reading experience that will leave you breathless.

WWW.ELLORASCAVE.COM

Printed in the United States
30771LVS00003B/67-633

9 781419 950513